CREATURES OF APPETITE

TODD TRAVIS

DARK MATTERS PRESS

CREATURES OF APPETITE

Todd Travis

INTRODUCTION

They call it the Heartland Child Murders. Everyone else calls it a nightmare. Locked doors don't stop him. He leaves no trace behind. He only takes little girls.

His nickname … **The Iceman**.

A deranged serial killer roams wintry rural Nebraska, targeting little girls, with a demented purpose no one can fathom.

FBI Special Agent **EMMA KANE**, a former DC cop considered to be damaged goods, is assigned to babysit burned-out profiler **JACOB THORNE** as they both fly to Nebraska to catch this maniac.

Thorne is erratic, abrasive and unpredictably brilliant, but what he and Kane find in the heartland is much more than anyone bargained for, especially when the Iceman challenges them personally, where it hurts most.

The clock is ticking and a little girl's life is on the line. And maybe even more with that, once they find out what he's really up to.

REVIEWS

"You're used to clever plots, complex characters, twisted cases and brilliant writing. Few things can surprise you, because most times you figure out who the murderer is before the book ends. Well, let me tell you something: 'Creatures of Appetite' by Todd Travis is like nothing you've read before.Prepare yourself to be hooked from the very first pages, to forget that you need to eat or sleep, and to be taken by surprise by a twisted ending that you could have never guessed." -- **Jo Ammons, NY Books Examiner**

"If you start reading this book thinking that you'll be able to put it down before bedtime, you're wrong. You'll only be able to fall asleep after you turn the last page. Usually, readers who read a lot of crime novels gain the ability to guess how everything is going to end, or at least suspect. It's not going to happen with "Creatures of Appetite",because the ending will come as a shock." -- **Top Books Worth Reading**

"No, as a reader you won't guess who the murderer is before Jacob

Thorne puts two and two together, but that's not what makes Creatures of Appetite stand out in its genre. What makes it really worth reading is on the very last pages." --**All Fantasy Worlds**

Over eight hundred five-star reviews on Amazon!

Leave your review there today!

COPYRIGHT

Cover illustration by

Bosa Grgurevic: www.Buddhacandy.com

For the darkness, that black bastard in us all ... I ain't scared of you, not no more.

CHAPTER 1

M aureen dragged her daughter Tami through the crowded outdoor flea market on the hunt for a deal. Snow fell, covering the school parking lot, the entire market, customers and vendors alike, but that stopped no one. In Nebraska during the winter, snow fell nearly every other day, but the flea market was but once a month.

And no one looked forward to it more than Maureen. While some women were addicted to soap operas, some to pills and others to Facebook, Maureen's drug of choice was secondhand sales.

It wasn't from economical necessity, for her husband Richard was a good provider with a decent job and good benefits. It was simply that the search for bargains was Maureen's personal primal urge. Each find a treasure, each dollar saved a victory, and as a result very few items in Maureen's household were brand new, except for her husband's golf clubs and, of course, everyone's underwear.

Even Richard, divorced when he met Maureen ten years earlier, would remark that she'd been primarily interested in

1

him because he was used goods, but he smiled when he said that. And it was easy for him to have a sense of humor about it, since he wasn't forced to accompany Maureen on her excursions as Tami was.

Tami, only five years old and definitely not used goods, was very much bored by it all, the flea market, the yelling and especially the constant pulling from place to place. Tami eyed the nearly empty school playground and yanked at her mother's hand.

"Mommy, swings!"

"Hush, Tami, Mommy's busy."

Maureen spotted a marked-down crock-pot and released Tami's hand to beat two other housewives to it. Finally free, Tami took advantage and made for the playground, away from the crowd and the noise as Maureen argued with her competitors.

Tami wandered over to the swings, her boots crunching in the snow, and gave each one a push to watch it go back and forth. She noticed two boys, a couple of years older than her, next to the jungle gym on the other end of the playground. The boys beckoned Tami over and she shyly joined them.

"You wanna see something really scary?" the larger of the two asked, frozen mucous crusted on his upper lip.

Tami nodded, proud to be included in the activities of the older children. The smaller boy, a scarf wrapped around his lower face so that only his eyes could be seen, pointed a snow-covered mitten into the shadows underneath the jungle gym.

"Tami!" Maureen called out over the crowd but the children paid no attention.

Tami wasn't quite able to make out what was on the ground. She slipped under the gym bars to get a closer look. The boys stayed right where they were.

"Tami Sue Paulson!" Maureen yelled, more frantic and closer now.

Tami finally got near enough for a good look at it and stopped right in her tracks. She put her mitten-covered thumb into her mouth, her eyes wide as saucers. Maureen, Crock-Pot tucked under one arm, marched over to the jungle gym.

"Tami Sue Paulson, how many times do I have to tell you about wandering off-"

Maureen stopped. The Crock-Pot fell from her hands and broke on the ground. Her face froze in mid-sentence for an instant, and then melted into a horrendous scream.

The two boys gawked, shocked at the volume of noise the grown-up was able to produce. Tami didn't even acknowledge her mother, just sucked her thumb and stared at the object, or rather objects, on the ground.

In the shadows, a child's foot lay, frozen and bare. Another foot, mate to the first, was also in the vicinity on the ground but at enough distance away to suggest that the two feet were no longer joined together by a body.

Maureen screamed and screamed as her daughter simply sucked her own thumb, unable to look away from the pieces of a dead child's body on the playground.

CHAPTER 2

Special Agent Emma Kane forced herself to stop pacing and instead leaned against the dark sedan double-parked outside the auditorium on Eleventh Avenue. A few homeless people eyed her as they scavenged through the trash for empty cans and other forgotten treasures. She eyed them right back. She'd never liked New York City.

Kane, thirty-three with dark hair, deep blue eyes and the natural build of an athlete, was considered by many to be an attractive woman, but Kane herself considered her looks, as well as those who considered her looks, to be of secondary importance in the grand scheme of things. Kane did what she could to underplay it, wore conservative clothes and shoes, avoided skirts and jewelry and of course never put on makeup. But she got attention anyway and hated it with every fiber of her being.

Her right foot tapped on the ground several times unconsciously like a mad puppet until she caught herself at it.

Nerves, I'm nervous, Kane thought, I can't be nervous. I'm

on my first assignment and I'm about to meet a legend. Nervousness not allowed, she told herself.

Kane reflected on her status as a special agent for the Federal Bureau of Investigation, effective all of six days. She was fresh from Quantico and didn't want it to show. It wasn't as though she were an untested rookie, after all. She was a seasoned investigator with a drawer full of citations and even a medal.

A cop in DC for twelve years, she started out as a uniform and spent her last eight years as a detective in Homicide, where she'd done very well. Her rise in the ranks, even before The Van Incident, had been stellar due to her natural smarts and hard work. Peers whispered, behind Kan's back, that her good fortune had as much to do with her physical attributes as her close rate, but that was just jealous bullshit gossip.

Kane saw the smirks and heard the rumors, of course, but ignored them while systematically closing case after case. She loved the work, loved the long hours, most of all she loved being in the right, which was how she thought of the law. The law was about fighting for what was right, standing up for it no matter what. Once she'd made up her mind in regard to what was right and what was not, Kane was unbendable, which oftentimes put her at odds with her superiors.

That attitude, Kane's looks, her disinterest in socializing with other cops and her cold temper made her less than popular within the division. The rumor that she was on the fast track to Internal Affairs didn't help, either.

Though heavily recruited, Kane had no interest in IAD; she liked the street, but once tagged as IAD fodder, the label was hard to get rid of. She'd had three partners in her eight years in Homicide and hadn't been close to any of them. Her first two partners were older married men and very careful not to get too familiar with her, lest it might lead to rumors that could wreck their marriages and careers.

Her last partner was female and the worst of the bunch; she could barely speak to Kane without a sneer on her face. The woman, an experienced detective with the air of a tough biker grandmother, often acted offended by Kane's very existence within the department. Kane shouldered it all, the snickers and whispered comments, her partner's disdain, caught up in the work.

This was all before The Van Incident, as she liked to refer to her last Homicide case in DC. It was easier for her to think of it that way, in her head it was always The Van Incident in capital letters; somehow that made it less raw and painful despite the acclaim and honor the case brought her.

After The Van Incident, her partner no longer treated Kane with barely masked annoyance; her partner and almost everyone in her division looked at her with only guilt and pity. Kane preferred the annoyance and disdain. An opportunity to go federal presented itself during the media circus afterward and she leapt for it.

And here she was, a federal officer.

Kane spotted an object on the ground in the alley between the auditorium and the building next to it. It broke her out of her reverie and made her blood rush.

The object appeared to be flesh-colored.

Kane moved into the alley fast and headed for what looked like a small, bare white foot lying on the ground in the alley, covered in trash. Catching her breath, Kane crouched down and carefully moved the trash out of the way with a pen, revealing a broken toy doll, missing the other leg and foot.

A toy. It was just a toy. Kane stared at it a moment and exhaled slowly. Jumpy, she thought, not only am I nervous, I'm also jumpy.

Kane stood and walked back down the alley toward her sedan, frustrated with herself. Three tough-looking Hispanic men on their way down the sidewalk filled the alley exit to the street. They chattered back and forth with each other until they saw Kane standing in the alley. They stopped to stare. The largest whistled and the short one made an obscene gesture with his tongue.

"Oh Mommy," said the man in the middle. They didn't move from where they stood, in essence blocking Kane's way out.

Kane shook her hair out of her eyes and continued out of the alley. The men didn't move out of her way and Kane had to pass close as they openly leered. A small ball of anger and fear festered in the pit of her stomach. At the last second, before she stepped completely past them, the largest man winked to his friends, reached down and grabbed a handful of Kane's ass.

Kane grabbed the big man's hand quick and twisted, putting him into a wristlock. He yelled in pain and went down on his knees. The two remaining men took a threatening step but the business end of Kane's automatic pistol stopped them. The barrel of her gun shook, just a bit.

"I don't think your mothers would be very proud of you right at this moment," Kane said. "But maybe they wouldn't give a shit, because if this is the way you treat women, then they didn't do a very good job of raising you."

"Fuck you," spit one of the men, following that with a torrent of obscene Spanish.

"Fuck you right back," Kane replied in Spanish as she cocked her pistol. "Next time you get the urge to grab the ass of a woman you don't know, bear in mind that she is also somebody's daughter, somebody's sister and someday somebody's mother.

"Would you like it if somebody grabbed your mother's

ass?" Kane twisted the big man's wrist to underline her point and he grunted in pain.

The men held up their hands and backed away slowly. Kane released the big guy and stepped back. He crawled away from her until he was able to stand and join his friends, rubbing his wrist painfully. Kane kept her weapon trained upon the three men.

The point of her pistol wavered and shook noticeably. The men noticed, exchanged knowing grins with each other before they turned tail down the street.

"Pricks," Kane took a deep breath and holstered her weapon. She looked at her still-shaking weapon hand. She took another deep breath and gritted her teeth, willing the shakes to stop. Finally her hand stilled. Kane returned to the sedan.

It's kind of funny, she thought, I used to like pimp-slapping punks that deserve it. Punks like them. Not now.

Now it just gave her the shakes.

Now it only brought her back to a place she'd rather not recall.

CHAPTER 3

I nside the auditorium, a silent but very engaged audience observed a massive chess tournament that had just begun. Two long rows of tables and chessboards ran parallel to each other on the auditorium floor, each board with its own player, seated on the outside, perched and ready to rumble, chess style.

The Grandmaster, a spry old man with long grey hair held back in a ponytail, walked the center of the floor, going down one row of boards and up the other, making fast moves against opponents who were obviously no match for him.

On his third lap around, near the end of the second row, the Grandmaster stopped, disturbed by the layout he saw on that particular board. The Grandmaster thought about it, and then slowly sat down at the chessboard to give the situation his full attention.

An excited murmur raced through the audience. This never happened, the old man never sat down, never. Heads craned to see who the Grandmaster's opponent was.

Jacob Thorne watched the Grandmaster calmly from

across the chessboard, chewing bubblegum. Thorne, in his late forties, was unremarkable in appearance, enough so that once you saw him you were apt to forget what he looked like almost immediately. Unless Thorne opened his mouth and spoke. Once he opened his mouth, he usually made a very memorable and lasting impression. Very pleased with himself, Thorne blew a bubble and winked at the Grandmaster.

Come on, old man, Thorne thought. Come get the candy.

Something caught Thorne's attention up in the audience stands. A man in the bleachers stared plainly at Thorne and held up a large white tablet.

Printed on it in black marker, the words "I NEED YOU."

Thorne shook his head at the man in the stands and focused back on the board. The Grandmaster finally made his move and stood back up. Thorne countered immediately and the Grandmaster sat back down to consider the new situation.

Thorne glanced up again. This time the tablet read: "IT'S IMPORTANT."

The Grandmaster made another move and Thorne countered immediately. The Grandmaster moved again and Thorne countered yet again, putting the Grandmaster on the run. The Grandmaster sat quietly a moment, stumped. Thorne didn't want to look up at the audience but couldn't help himself.

On the tablet, the word "PLEASE" printed in very large letters. Thorne sighed and cursed silently under his breath. With a shrug, he tipped his king over and ceded the game to The Grandmaster. A murmur went through the watchful audience. The Grandmaster, surprised, stood and held out his hand to shake but was spurned as Thorne walked out of the auditorium without a backward glance.

The man from the bleachers, Peter Viera, found Thorne

waiting for him in the lobby. Viera held up the tablet again. It read "THANK YOU."

"Cute," Thorne grunted. "Cute, deliberate and slick as shit. Ivy League nickel-and-dime-store pysch-fuckery, as usual."

"Worked though, didn't it?" Viera tossed the tablet to one side.

"We'll see. What do you want? This better be important. You know how long I've been waiting to trap that gray-haired prick in there? This better be rock-star fucking important."

"Would I come all the way here by myself if it weren't important?"

"You might, yes."

"You haven't returned our calls or emails. Most of the time we can't even locate you."

"I don't want to be located. What do you want?"

"In case you haven't noticed, we've been a little busy ourselves."

"I haven't noticed, Pete, I don't care anymore."

"If I really believed that, I wouldn't have come all the way up here on my own just to talk to you."

"You really think that you're here alone? If that's true, then who were the two guys in the auditorium watching you watch me?"

"My shadows. I figured you'd make them. But officially, I'm the only one here to talk to you, no one else. The feeling was that, if we sent anyone else, you would have just said no without even hearing them out."

"And who says I won't do the same to you?"

"You might. But it's been noted that you tolerate me more than most and I hope that you will at least talk to me."

"I'm talking, aren't I? What do you want? I've asked you three fucking times."

"Jake, we want you back."

"We do? We-who? WE as in you and a couple guys who want a consult on something or WE as in the director, MacVey and the Bureau? Which kind of WE are we talking about here?"

"We as in the Bureau."

"The Bureau wants me back, the whole fucking Bureau, the whole house of cards, that's the WE that wants me back?"

"The WE that makes these kinds of decisions do," Viera replied. "They want you back with a badge."

"Why? You don't need me, you're loaded with profilers, psych-shrinks and forensic specialists."

"Not like you, you're different. You're ahead of the curve. That's why I badgered the director into bringing you back."

Thorne fixed him with a look that, Viera would later swear, was a hell of a lot more intimidating than any polygraph he knew of. Thorne sniffed.

"And he said yes?"

"He said yes. He wasn't happy about it, but he said yes."

"I'll bet he wasn't happy. Prick."

"You did tell him to go fuck himself, Jake."

"Say I do come back. To do what?"

"Case in Nebraska called the Heartland Child Murders."

"Not the Mercy Killings?" Thorne asked.

"The Heartland Child Murders."

"Never heard of it."

"You're serious, you haven't heard anything?"

"I don't read the papers or watch the news. I told you, I stopped caring once I got the gold watch."

"It's a bad one. It's taken a backseat in the media from the insanity of the Mercy Killings, but it's there and it's real bad. Twenty-two kids missing, nine confirmed dead, all little girls, ages five to twelve."

"Kids, huh?"

"Papers are calling him the Iceman."

"Whose bright-eyed fucking idea was that?"

"Some dickhead television reporter, I don't know, the name stuck and there isn't anything we can do about it."

"Iceman," Thorne snorted.

"He's definitely got balls, of that we have no doubt. He waltzes in and takes kids right from under their parents' noses. He's done this without breaking a sweat or losing his cool. We don't even find any trace of them most of the time. We have remains on nine of the victims, but even then they're not whole, he leaves a leg here or an arm or head there."

"You sure it's a he?"

"You tell me. Most profilers agree our subject is male, but you tell me, that's why I want you on this. Talk to me, could it be a female?"

"Don't know. Won't know until I get a look at the file, if I decide I even want to."

"It's a nasty one, he snatches them, parts them out and leaves little forensics when doing so. Jake, this is not even funny, it's evil and ugly and it absolutely has got to be stopped. We're behind the curve on it and we need help."

"The Heartland Child Murders," Thorne mused.

"I need you, Jake, I need you to work your magic on this case."

"I was working my goddamn magic on the Mercy Killings when MacVey and the director shoved a gold watch up my ass, Pete."

"I know they did and you know how I felt about it at the time. That's why I'm here now. I need your game on this, Jake, it's turned into a real fucking hairball. The Task Force commander is a homegrown corn-fed cop who can't find his ass in the dark with both hands; all he's thinking about is press conferences and who's going play his part in the movie version of this whole shitstorm.

"The local profilers are lost and the agent we had advising them, Riggs, was nursing a divorce and a drinking problem that we didn't know about. He had a breakdown and fucked the whole thing up. I need you on this. Take the badge and bring them home.

"You may have stopped caring but I bet you haven't stopped missing the chase. You miss it, Jake, I know you do. You know you're the MAN on this kind of show, you're my star and I need you in the game. Catch this sick bastard. We can't let this turn into another JonBenet Ramsey fuck-up, this is over twenty kids we're talking about here. It's as big or bigger than Atlanta ever was."

"Big but not the biggest."

"What do you want, Jake?"

"What do you think I want?"

"All right," Viera said after a moment, "take the Heartland Child Murders, help them close it and close it fast. You do that for me and I'll get you what you want. I'll get you back on the Mercy Killings."

"No shit?"

"No shit."

"No way MacVey would ever agree to that, he wouldn't even let me in the same fucking room as him, no way."

"MacVey's dead, Jake."

"Dead?"

"Dead. Got it same way as Mueller and Cosmo."

"Holy fucking shit," Thorne had to sit to think about this. "Okay. Now you have my attention."

"Nobody, NOBODY knows about this, we've kept it out of the media, it's even kept out of the official reports by order of the director and the president himself. Story is just like it was the first time, we got their families cooperating,

14

everything. This goes no farther than you and me. When it's over and done and we got the fucker, then we'll bury our own proper. Until then we say nothing. We have a national frenzy going on as it is, if word got out about this it might lead to a complete breakdown."

"So who's running the Mercy Killings now?"

"I'm the new SAC. The director and the president want the Mercy Killings closed fucking yesterday, top priority. I'm going to do that. But I need you to catch this Iceman, he's killing goddamn little kids, Jake. Even the Mercy Killer doesn't target kids. I need you to stop him right-fucking-immediately."

"I close the kid case, I get another shot at the Mercy Killings. Your word?"

"My word," Viera said. "If I don't close it first, you get your shot at it."

Thorne stood and offered his hand to Viera. They shook hands.

"I always liked you, Pete."

"Just catch him, unleash that Jacob Thorne voodoo and catch this cute cocksucker. I got a plane waiting for you, let's go."

"First Mueller and Cosmo, then MacVey," Thorne picked up his coat and followed Viera out of the lobby. "You're up at bat. That what the shadows are for?"

"We have shooters watching me everywhere I go, I am watched constantly, I can't even shit by myself anymore. The director is hoping that if the Mercy Killer is tempted to make a run at me next, we'll nail him."

"How nice, a big fucking target on your back, you gotta like that. Where would you rate your ass-pucker factor these days?"

"On a scale from one to ten? Eleven."

CHAPTER 4

Thorne and Viera exited the front doors of the auditorium and made their way to the street where Kane stood against the sedan.

"She's not one of your shooters. This your secretary or what?"

"Didn't I mention? There's a catch," Viera allowed himself to smile for the first time this day. "You have to work with a partner on this one."

"What? No fucking way."

"That's the deal. She's a top investigator out of DC, just joined ISU."

"Pete, have you lost your fucking mind?"

Kane stepped forward to meet them.

"Special Agent Emma Kane, Jacob Thorne."

"Agent Thorne, I'm a big admirer of your work," Kane held out her hand.

"Honey, I don't need any blow-job groupies, understand? Goddamn it, Pete-"

"It's the only way the director would agree to bringing you back," Viera replied. "It's non-negotiable. We don't let anyone work alone anymore, not with what's been happening."

"No fucking way, I work alone or forget it."

"Come on, Jake, don't put me there. This is how it is. Remember MacVey? Nobody works alone anymore, nobody. You have to have a partner, and I figured you'd prefer to have a rookie who doesn't know anything as opposed to a veteran who's going to constantly butt heads with you. Think about it, it's much better this way. You take her along, show her the ropes. She's a good cop, she's been proven under fire. That's the deal, Jake, take it."

Kane stared at the two of them, stoic. Thorne glared at Viera. Finally Thorne kicked the sedan fender with a curse.

"Shit. Great, just great. You set me up, you bastard. You get me hooked, get my mind on the game again and you stick me with a goddamn Girl Scout!"

"Agent Thorne, it's the twenty-first century. Women have long been recognized as being just as capable as men," Kane said, fire in her eyes.

"Great, she's a feminist with issues, too. I'm going to get you for this, Pete."

"You've always said it was the brains and balls that count," Viera reminded him.

"Key word, balls, key word."

"What's wrong with him, is he in the middle of a raging mid-life crisis or something?" Kane said.

Viera liked that. "No, he's always been this way. Probably popped out of the womb exactly as you see him now."

"I can't believe this. She looks like a fucking refugee from the Playboy channel," Thorne spit out his gum.

"Hey, I'm right here, you got something to say about me then say it directly to my face, don't talk over my head like I don't exist, clear? And I suggest that you can this woman shit right here and now, it's old and it's tired," Kane said. "It's a long proven fact that women can do anything men can do. We can even pee standing up if we choose."

"If that's true, how often do you do it?"

"I'll do whatever I have to do to catch this shitbird, even if it means pissing on you. Got it?"

"I can tell right now that this is going to be interesting," Viera said as they all climbed into the sedan.

CHAPTER 5

"What do you know about Jacob Thorne?" Viera had asked Kane earlier on the plane to New York.

Kane had of course heard of Thorne, he was much discussed at the academy, especially when his retirement was announced while she was at Quantico. She'd also heard of him well before going federal, back when she was a cop, and not all that she'd heard about him was good. She took a moment to decide how much to say or not to say.

"A few things. I know that he's a profiler, been with the Bureau for years. He's a legend, that's how I've heard him described. A legend. Some say he's the best there is," Kane replied.

"The some that say that are exactly right."

"We studied some of his case files in class at Quantico, the work he's done is impressive, to say the least. Very smart. A lot of the instructors talk about him, but …"

"But what?"

"But … I don't know, they don't really say much about him, I don't know how else to put it. We hear quite a bit about some of the Old School profilers, study their cases so closely we almost get to know the man himself in addition to the work he did. Not true with Thorne. It was hard to get a picture of who he was just from the case studies. Even the instructors that talked about him didn't seem to really know him.

"Also, most of the other retired guys come back and lecture, tell us stories, you know the drill. Thorne's never done that."

Viera acknowledged that with a grunt. "Nor will he. You ever meet him?"

"No. I've heard stories, especially back on the job. They flew him down to DC to consult on the sniper shootings. The skinny was that the information he gave the commander was of considerable help in the end.

"Thorne was the first to suggest that there was more than one killer and that our subjects were black. No one else had suggested that up to that point. Some in the division were opposed to that view; in fact, opposed would probably be too polite a word. Race relations in DC have never been very good, and it was feared that suggesting to the public that we had not one, but two, black serial killers without solid evidence backing that up could possibly make things worse."

"And what was Thorne's response to that?"

"I heard, I don't know for sure, but I heard that Thorne suggested to the chief that having his head up his own ass, as the chief obviously did, couldn't make things any worse than they already were. I only heard the rumor, I don't know if it really happened."

"Sounds about his speed," Viera grunted.

"It was also said that after the subjects were caught, the brass tried to contact him in order to offer congratulations, give him credit, and he told them to keep his name out of it and not to bother him again."

"Yeah, he does that, too. Anything else?"

"At Quantico it was said that Thorne burned out on the Mercy Killings and had to retire, that's what the word was."

"He burned, but I don't know that I would characterize it as a burning out, but he definitely burned something, especially a lot of bridges. No, he may have crashed but he sure as hell didn't burn out. Don't let the retirement fool you, the day he left he was still as sharp as a fucking tack, I doubt he's lost anything in his game.

"But even if it were true and he did burn out, it would be hard to blame him for that, because the Mercy Killings are the biggest pain in the balls case this country has ever had. More than a few good men have burned out on that twisted fucking cocksucker already, burned out and then some."

It was a curious thing to say and Kane wanted to ask him to explain further, but something in Viera's tone cautioned her against it. It was also, she noted, the very first time Viera cursed in front of her, not casual polite cursing either, but the true blue coarse language favored by cops everywhere.

Serious cursing was an act usually avoided by your average federal officer who, in their dry-cleaned dark jackets, ironed white shirts and dark ties, were courteous and polite to the point of obscenity itself. This was their history since Hoover, and Kane had yet to meet a fed who swore like a good cop can, especially a fed as high up on the food chain in the Bureau as Peter Viera.

When she first met Viera, Kane thought he had the air of a tough high school principal, the kind of disciplinarian that came down hard on unruly behavior yet could be counted on as a dependable shoulder to lean on when real trouble arrived. Now Kane realized that she couldn't have been more mistaken.

"The Mercy Killings," Viera said, looking Kane right in the eye, "are a fucking national disaster and that may even be understating the situation, but it didn't burn Thorne out. And don't ask me anything regarding that case, I couldn't tell you even if I wanted to."

Viera must have read her mind, because Kane would have loved to gotten some dirt on the Mercy Killings. The one thing cops liked to do more than curse was gossip, especially about the Mercy Killings, the most sensational serial killer in the history of the form with over two hundred victims across the country. The whole world was watching, waiting to see where he'd strike next.

"Keep in mind," Viera said, "you're working on the Heartland Child Murders, that's what you requested, that's why you are here. Don't waste a minute thinking about the Mercy Killer, that's my problem. I want you eating, sleeping and shitting one thing and one thing only, the Heartland Child Murders. That is the single solitary object on your plate. Are we clear on that?"

"We're very clear," Kane replied.

"It better be. Now I want to tell you a few things about Jacob Thorne. He's an arrogant, touchy bastard. That's what I think and I like him more than anyone else in the Bureau. He's never been a cop, came straight into the Bureau from college and drifted over into Behavioral Sciences mainly because it was new at the time and he couldn't get along with anyone anywhere else. Behavioral Sciences was what they called that division in the beginning, they later changed the name to Investigative Support Unit primarily because everyone kept referring to it as the BS Unit, bullshit central, which drove the elders nuts. Thorne did really well there in spite of himself. He'd be running ISU if he could just get along with people.

"He pushes buttons on everyone, and usually the wrong ones, just for the hell of it. He's not a shrink, he's not a forensic scientist, thinks police procedure is a waste of time and that he's a lot fucking smarter than anyone else. He might even be right about the last one. He's a legend for a reason, Kane, he's a genius when it comes to catching psychopaths.

"I'm very good at what I do, but I couldn't tell you how he does what he does, I just know that he can do it and do it better than I can. He gets in their heads until he finds them. Sometimes he gives us our guy and we can't prove it, but he's always right. If it weren't for the mess the Mercy Killings was making of our reputation ... never mind that.

"He's the best I've ever seen, bar none, and I've seen everyone. The two guys that started Behavioral Sciences with him went on to write books, go on talk shows, advise for the movies and all that shit, now regular people know who they are. Not Thorne, he truly doesn't give a fuck about that.

"He's got an ego, make no mistake, but he really doesn't care about the credit on his cases, he doesn't like any attention from the media, none of that shit. He just likes the challenge. The guy lives in his head and it must be a fucking fascinating place. I wouldn't know because I've never been there and I don't know that I'd even want to go. One thing I will tell you. If you want to know everything there is to know about catching homicidal psychos, Thorne is the guy that can show you, so pay close attention to what he has to say."

"Yes, sir."

"One last thing. I may not be able to get him to come back. It's going to be touch and go, he has to be dealt with very delicately. But if I do get him back on the job, I guarantee that he will not like working with you and he'll be a flaming asshole about it. He will get under your skin, he'll look into your bowels, pull something out that will fuck with you and piss you off; that's what he does.

"That's why he's a legend and why the suits we all work for hate him. Be ready for it and whatever you do, do not ever just eat his shit, you know what I'm saying? Give as good as you get, do not back down from him. Got it?"

Kane took a moment to make sure her voice was steady before she spoke.

"Yes, sir. I got it."

"You'd better. Because everything you know or think you know about this job is about to change, starting right now today."

CHAPTER 6

K elly woke suddenly. She'd heard something. Even though she'd been fast asleep, she was certain she'd heard something. A creaking noise from somewhere in her house. She poked Bryan, who grunted but didn't move. Kelly caught her breath and listened hard to what the house had to say for itself. It could be that she dreamt it, the noise. There, she heard it again. It sounded almost like footsteps and that frightened her. Kelly reached over to her husband and shook him.

"Bryan," Kelly whispered. "Bryan! I hear something."

"It's the furnace," Bryan didn't even open his eyes. "Go back to sleep."

"It's NOT the furnace, listen," Kelly shook him again. "Wake up and listen!"

"Woman, would you just …" Bryan stopped suddenly. He'd heard something himself. Bryan grabbed his glasses from the nightstand next to the bed and put them on. He held a hand up to his wife to quiet her as he sat up. They listened together again to their house, which now had nothing to say for itself. Now Bryan didn't care for the

25

silence of his house, it was almost like his home had been whispering and somehow gotten shushed. Bryan swung out of bed, barefoot in sweatpants and a T-shirt.

"Did you check on Wendy before bed?"

"Yes, like always," Kelly whispered. "She was out like a light, you know she always sleeps hard after swimming. What is it?"

"It's probably nothing. I'm gonna check on Wendy. You stay here."

Bryan padded over to their closed bedroom door. He paused before opening it, reached down and grabbed the baseball bat right next to the bedroom closet. With everything going on, he and Kelly had been taking care never to let their daughter Wendy, who was nine, out of their sight at any time outside of their house. They took turns waiting for her after her school functions and she never went anywhere without one of her parents close by.

In addition, he'd started keeping his trusty baseball bat close by the bed when he slept, which made him feel better even though the house was bolted up tight at night. He had a shotgun in the house as well, most folks in Nebraska did, but that was kept locked up downstairs in the cabinet. He couldn't very well leave a loaded shotgun lying around his bedroom because Wendy was in the habit of walking in her sleep and sometimes he and Kelly would wake up to find her snuggled in bed between them.

They couldn't take the chance that she might pick the weapon up, even in her sleep. As he listened at the door to the hallway, Bryan thought to himself, just for a brief moment, that maybe it was time to move the whole damn gun cabinet into their bedroom.

He hoped Wendy had another case of the night-walks, gotten up to go to the bathroom for a glass of water or to pee, and that was all it was.

"Bryan!"

"Shhh!"

Bryan slowly cracked the bedroom door open and looked out into the hall. Nothing. He opened it all the way and stepped quietly out into the hall, listening very hard to his house as it slept.

A small night-light cast a bit of illumination around the hall and the rest of the second floor. Bryan tiptoed to the railing of the stairs and looked down into the first floor. Everything was quiet and covered in shadow. Nothing moved or made noise. Bryan walked quietly toward his daughter's bedroom, hefting his bat to calm his nerves. Bryan slowly opened his daughter's door and stepped in, bat held high.

Under the blue glow of her Lilo and Stitch night-light, his daughter Wendy slept, curled up blissfully in her bed. Bryan breathed a sigh of relief and lowered his bat. He gently moved an errant blonde hair that had fallen into Wendy's mouth and adjusted the covers on her bed. Can't be too careful these days with all the insanity going on in the world, Bryan thought as he watched his daughter sleep.

Bryan returned to his bedroom and his wife a few moments later, shut their bedroom door and tossed his bat back to its spot next to his closet.

"Is she ..." Kelly whispered.

"Wendy's fine, I just checked on her, sleeping like a baby."

Bryan yawned, put his glasses on the nightstand and crawled back into bed.

"Is everything ..."

"Everything's cool, I went downstairs, checked everything out, house is still locked up, nobody there, nothing to worry about."

"Then what was it?"

"Just the house, houses make noise as they settle for the winter. Don't worry, honey-bunny."

Bryan turned off the lamp next to the bed and settled back under the covers. Kelly snuggled up close to her husband. "My hero." They cuddled for a few moments. "Bryan. Bryan?"

"What?"

"I'm thirsty."

"So go get a drink of water."

"You're already up. Bryan? Bryyyan. I'll make it worth your while. Bryan?"

"Damn, Kelly! All right, okay."

Bryan grabbed his glasses and slid out of bed again, this time without turning the light on. He stomped over to his bedroom door and opened it.

A tall man in black with a dark ski mask pulled over his head stood in the bedroom doorway. The Iceman.

Before Bryan could speak or react, the Iceman quickly touched him on the side of his neck with an electric stun gun, which sparked upon contact with Bryan's skin.

Bryan collapsed to the floor without a sound, unconscious.

Kelly turned toward the door at the sound of the Taser and squinted into the darkness of the bedroom before her.

Without a word, the Iceman stepped into the dark bedroom toward the fallen man's wife.

"Bryan?" Kelly whispered.

CHAPTER 7

Bad winter weather blanketing the Midwest made for a bouncy flight on the Bureau plane. Thorne hunched over the case file in his lap, oblivious to the turbulence. Kane walked unsteadily down the aisle and sat in the seat opposite him.

"What do you think so far?" Kane asked.

"I think that you should stay on the other side of the plane and not bother me," Thorne grunted.

"There's been another abduction."

"Where?" Thorne perked up.

"York, Nebraska," she handed over her iPad.

"York, Nebraska?" Thorne grabbed it. "Where the fuck is York, Nebraska?"

"Wendy Frederickson, nine years old," Kane recited from memory, "blonde, blue eyes, no distinguishing marks or scars. Taken from her bedroom. Parents left unconscious but alive and unharmed, they thought they heard someone in the house and when they went to investigate someone zapped them with a stun gun. They don't recall what he looked like, how big he was or any distinguishing characteristics. They

29

have very little memory of what happened once they woke up. Doors of the house were dead-bolted; everything was left locked just as it was before they went to bed.

"We don't know how he got in and we don't know how he got out. A few fibers, couple of scratches on the door, but other than that, no prints, nothing."

"Of course not," Thorne glanced at the emailed report for a moment before burying his head back into the file.

"We've hit a snowstorm, so we're going to be late in landing," Kane said.

Thorne grunted, not looking at her. Kane watched him for a bit before speaking again.

"I'd rather not fight with you on this, Agent Thorne. You've got one hell of a reputation. You have more letters of recommendation than anyone in the history of the Bureau."

"And more letters of censure."

"Some say you're the best there is."

"I'm one of them."

"If you're the best, then tell me," Kane leaned forward, "do you have any idea who this Iceman is yet?"

"Not WHO. Only WHAT."

"What?"

"That's right."

"What's right?"

"Exactly."

Kane thought about that. "You're saying that you don't know WHO he is, but you do know WHAT he is."

"Hey, look at that," Thorne looked up from the file, "she's not just a pair of tits and a smile."

"You've got a problem with women, I've noticed that. It must have been tough for you, leaving Hoover and the Eisenhower era behind."

"Hoover was a fag."

"I believe the official term was transvestite. Regardless, I think it's time for you to adjust to the situation, meaning, cease and desist the sexist bullshit effective immediately."

"What for?"

"What for? We're partners."

"We're not partners."

"We are partners."

"We are not partners, this isn't a buddy picture here. We're not Butch and Sundance, Starsky and Hutch or Freebie and Bean. We're not even Turner and Hooch. Get it straight. I'm here for one reason only. To close this case. No other reason. That's it. I am not here to Miyagi a fucking rookie who's been skating on her looks. Got it, Tootsie?"

Kane's eyes got hot.

"Let's get something straight here, bub," Kane leaned back. "My name is Kane, Special Agent Emma Kane with the Federal Bureau of Investigation, currently assigned to ISU National. Before that I did eight years with Homicide in DC. I closed cases. Women make you uncomfortable, attractive women especially, so I will apologize to you now for my clear skin and good bone structure, but never again. I'm not responsible for your insecurity. I closed cases, I closed tough cases, that's why the Bureau recruited me and that's why I got assigned to this case.

"I don't fucking skate, clear? You can dislike me or my gender, but you'd better recognize my ability and you'd better not ever call me Tootsie ever again, otherwise there is going to be a serious problem between the two of us. Now. Are you done trying to fuck with me?"

"You didn't get assigned on this case," Thorne said.

"Yes I did ..."

"You didn't, you requested this case. There's a difference."

"How did you know that?"

"I could tell you a lot about yourself if I thought it was worth the time, but what would be the point? You're a

31

major blue-flamer with a bug up your ass and personal issues, that much is painfully obvious," Thorne said. "Why this case?"

"Why not? I'm along for the ride, like it or not, why not show me some of what you can do?"

"Why should I help your career?"

"If career was all I cared about, I would have requested the Mercy Killings."

"And that's why I asked you, why this case?" Thorne pointed out.

"Someone's got to work it."

"Got a thing for kids, is that it?"

"Who doesn't have a thing for kids?"

"I don't."

"All right, it's true. I asked for this case. So what?"

"You see yourself as an avenger, is that it? Are you satisfying your maternal kicks trying to save kids?"

"I volunteered because it's a kid case and it's getting the short end of the stick."

"That's not the real reason."

"Sure it is."

"No, it's not, at least, that's not the real reason in specifics."

"It's little kids, what do you think ..."

"It's because it's little girls," Thorne cut her off. "That's what it is for you. Little girls. It fries you that he targets little girls and girls alone."

Kane didn't look away, but didn't deny it, either. "It needs the attention. Everyone else is focused on the Mercy Killings, which you were working before you decided to retire."

"I didn't retire. I was retired. There's a difference."

"Why were you retired?"

"Why should I tell you? You're so smart, you should be able to figure it out on your own."

"What is it, you couldn't handle it and they had to yank you, is that it?"

"If that's what you believe, why would you care what I think about this case?" Thorne asked as he leaned back, stretching his arms over his head with a yawn.

"I don't know what I believe yet, I just want to catch this killer, that's it, nothing else. I'd rather do it with you than without you. Come on. Show me your game."

Thorne fixed her with a gimlet eye for a moment, gazing down deep into her innards, as Kane would think of it later.

"You want in, profile me. Pitch it to me shorthand, the Jacob Thorne story."

"Shorthand?" Kane asked.

"Profile me, then maybe I'll play ball with you. Pitch me my profile, twenty-five words or less. Tell me. What am I?"

Kane mulled that challenge, her mind working fast.

"Cowboy. See yourself as Shane, riding into town to find Jack Palance, shoot his ass and get the fuck out of Dodge."

Thorne settled back into his seat, smiling and soaking that in for a moment.

"Shane?" Thorne said. "That's not bad. I like that. You even have three words to spare."

"Problem. With. Authority."

"Authority and I have no problems as long as authority recognizes that I am absolutely, always right."

"Am I in the game?" Kane asked.

Thorne thought for a long moment. Finally he shrugged and went back to his file.

"For now."

"So then tell me. What this killer is, why is that important?"

"It's the first step of the equation."

"What equation?"

"WHAT plus WHY equals WHO."

"So if we know WHAT he is …"

"And WHY he does what he does …"

"Then we know WHO. WHAT plus WHY equals WHO."

"Very good," Thorne said, "Miyagi have hope for you. Now leave me alone, I have work to do and I can't do it with you bending over me."

CHAPTER 8

Thorne and Kane finally landed in the city of Lincoln, the capital of Nebraska, later that day. Kane had had plenty of time while stuck on the plane to do some Internet research. Nebraska was 76,872 square miles in size, which made it the sixteenth largest state in the union just in terms of area. The last census put the population at 1,711,263. Factor area with that number and you got a population density of 22.3 people per square mile. Nebraska's nickname was the Cornhusker State. The state flower the goldenrod, the state bird the western meadowlark and the state motto, "Equality Before the Law."

Kane wasn't sure if any of this information would help, but she wasn't sure that it wouldn't, either. They hopped into a squad car and headed for Task Force Headquarters. Kane took a look around as they cut through the city, but it was hard to see anything through the falling snow.

Thorne simply closed his eyes, slumped down in the seat and ignored her. He hadn't said a word since their conversation on the plane and Kane was reluctant to speak and possibly lose what little ground she'd gained earlier, so she just let him be and stayed silent and kept surfing the net.

With a population of just under a quarter of a million souls, Lincoln was small, comparatively speaking, for a state capital, though its size and population grew significantly during the college school year, Lincoln being the home to the University of Nebraska. The university's football team, the Nebraska Cornhuskers, was extremely popular and it's reported that whenever a home game is played in the fall, the streets are deserted, with everyone either at the game or watching it on television.

A very clean city with wide sidewalks, friendly, helpful citizens and a low crime rate, it was considered the ideal place to raise a family. At least that's what the official city website read, the authors of which one would imagine were far from objective. Even the bars closed early, at one in the morning, which meant that last call was at twelve-thirty. In black and white on her laptop it felt a lot like Kane's home state of North Carolina, at least that was her first impression.

That impression lasted all of two seconds once she stepped outside and a below zero wind brought tears to her eyes. Thorne cursed the cold under his breath as they walked up the steps and into Task Force Headquarters.

Lieutenant Norman Hairston, an older man with obvious tendencies toward fussiness, stood waiting for them just inside headquarters and after introductions hurriedly led them through the maze of the main office area, peopled with large numbers of desks, cubicles, computers and men in uniform bustling about importantly.

"We expected you hours ago, did you get my email?" Hairston asked as he ushered them to a couple of empty desk cubicles in the corner.

"Yes I did, thank you, our plane was delayed by the snow-storm," Kane replied.

"The snow, yes, it is that time of year. Unfortunately, you've missed the morning briefing and there were one or two interesting developments. I've got a summary here somewhere, but first let me find the captain and introduce you. Andy, have you seen the captain?"

Andy, an officer in uniform, didn't look up from his desk where the report he worked on required as much concentration as he could reasonably spare. "He's in the can. He just went in, so he'll probably be awhile."

"Ah yes. The coffee hit. We're going to have you two situated at these desks here. Make yourselves at home and I'll see if I can arrange for someone to catch you up to where we are," Hairston bustled off.

Kane set her bag and coat down on the desk and gazed out the window. The amount of snow falling amazed her. A large map of Nebraska tacked up on one wall drew Thorne's attention. He examined it closely, pausing only to pop a fresh stick of gum into his mouth.

"Kane," Thorne said.

"What?" Kane swiveled quickly.

"Where are they putting us up, anyway?"

"Uh, I'm not sure. Budget Inn, I think."

"First class as usual," Thorne grunted, focused on the map on the wall. The abduction sites were all clearly marked on the map, crossing the state. Thorne followed them with his finger. Posted next to the map on a bulletin board were pictures of all the missing children.

Andy looked up from his paperwork to see Kane not even two feet away from him. He gawked openly at her.

"Are you really an FBI Agent?" Andy asked.

"I am," Kane looked at him sideways. "They gave me a real gun and everything."

As he studied the map on the wall, Thorne became aware of someone in a state trooper uniform standing next to him.

"Pretty sad, isn't it?"

"What is?" Thorne asked.

"This. We really should have caught someone by now, don't you think?"

"As long as it's the right someone, then yes, I do think that."

"Jeff Gilday, Nebraska State Patrol," Gilday held out his hand.

Thorne shook it, finding it to be a very strong handshake.

"Jacob Thorne."

"Pleased to meet you. Hey, Gerry! This is my buddy, Gerry Scroggins."

Another trooper, Scroggins, strolled over from behind a coffee machine. Scroggins and Gilday, both tall men in their thirties with the confident walk of an ex-athlete, checked out the new arrivals. Scroggins shook Thorne's hand, also inadvertently punishing Thorne's fist with yet another strong grip.

"Hey, how're ya doing? You the new Fibbie profiler?" Scroggins asked with a large friendly grin.

"Looks like it," Thorne freed his hand as soon as possible and silently resolved to avoid this exercise with anyone else in Nebraska. Kane walked over quickly and stuck her hand out to give it a go.

"How do you do, Special Agent Emma Kane," she said, giving Gilday a knuckle-cracking handshake in return. Gilday was not at all displeased at the sight of someone as attractive as Kane and neither was Scroggins. They also both found themselves quite fond of her grip, though neither would allow themselves to ruminate too much upon its potential, that being not the proper thing to do while in uniform.

"It is a definite pleasure," Scroggins said.

"Welcome to Nebraska."

"What's the state patrol's role in all of this?" Thorne asked.

"On loan to the Task Force, by special order of the governor, until this gets resolved."

"His Honor the governor wants this creep caught quick so he sent his two best to assist in the capture and that would be us," Scroggins said. "Pleased the Task Force captain to no end, you can bet. Not the most cooperative cop in the world, mostly lets us hang around as a liaison to the governor's office."

"Gerry, careful."

"What? It's true, isn't it?"

"Any thoughts on the situation?" Gilday asked Thorne.

"One or two," Thorne replied.

"You guys meet the captain yet?"

"Not yet," Kane said. "Apparently he's relieving himself."

"There's some good news," Scroggins said. "He's always a mean cuss until he's had his afternoon shit."

Captain Forsythe approached with Hairston whispering close into his ear. A large, red-faced, jowly man of fifty who looked like he should be wearing sideburns even though he wasn't, Forsythe was probably a big Elvis fan, Kane thought almost as a reflex. He glared at them.

"You two are late. I despise tardiness. And you want to know what I despise more than tardiness?'

"Passing notes in class?" Thorne asked. Forsythe looked at him for a moment, a hard look Kane was sure that Forsythe practiced in the bathroom mirror every morning. Forsythe cleared his throat and continued speaking.

"I despise having so-called experts shoved into my investigation against my will. I hate and despise that. We have our own people here and they are fully capable of handling this situation.

"The last clown you guys sent here, Riggs, turned the

whole investigation into one large Chinese clusterfuck and that's why he's gone. I will not allow that to happen again. Your role here, in case you haven't yet been told, is one of support. Nothing else. The FBI is not in charge of this case, I am.

"The governor of this state has entrusted me with catching this sick fuck and I will not let two glamour-seeking federal fuckheads get in my way. Make no mistake; I am the Big Dog on this case. My personal opinion of what you paper-pushing academics do is that it's mostly cable movie bullshit, but if by some twist of fate you DO have something of value to offer to this investigation, I will sit down with you later tonight and hear you out, but right now I have a press conference. Until then, just sit in the corner, fill out your little reports and stay the fuck out of my people's way."

Forsythe swiveled and stalked off, adjusting his tie as Hairston followed. Kane and Thorne looked at each other.

"I'm sure glad we caught him after his afternoon shit," Kane said.

CHAPTER 9

Kane discovered something new about herself when she arrived at Task Force Headquarters. She discovered that being among so many uniformed men and women made her feel very comfortable.

Even as a detective in Homicide, though she didn't wear one herself, she'd spent a lot of her time around the uniforms at the station. She hadn't realized that she missed it, spending time with uniformed cops, and even though she'd never been terribly social all throughout her enforcement career, the sight of the uniform triggered something in her. It fostered a feeling of safety and security somewhere deep in her soul.

A native of North Carolina, Kane had originally gone to college to become a doctor. She spent two years pre-med at Georgetown University before making the big switch to pre-law. An incident in her dorm during the start of her junior year triggered the switch.

As a dorm Resident Assistant, Kane was making a late night round in the hallway one Saturday night when she happened across one of her floor residents in a hot argument with her boyfriend. Seeing as that it was after curfew, those hours that members of the opposite sex were allowed on the floor, and that the young girl's boyfriend had her pinned by the throat against the hallway wall, Kane had no choice but to intervene. It was her job as Resident Assistant, after all, to deal with these types of situations, Kane thought quite calmly at the time. Kane grabbed the young man's arm and told him quite firmly to let the girl go. It did not go well from there.

The boyfriend, the star center on the college basketball team, took exception to her interference and expressed it by backhanding Kane roughly, knocking her to the ground. Her lip bleeding, Kane could taste both blood and shock. Did he hit me? she thought at the time, did he? Did he actually hit me? The question echoed in her mind nonstop as the young giant redirected his anger and rage from his girlfriend onto Kane.

Although Kane hadn't considered herself sheltered, as a straight A student with loving parents and good manners, as an attractive girl who didn't rebel through puberty, smoke, drink, stay out too late or do anything other than her home-work, Kane realized at that very moment, that she was, in fact, very sheltered.

Up to that point in life, she had never really witnessed or experienced any type of violence to her person other than the occasional "excuse me" type of bump in the hallway before class. In fact, males of all ages tended to exert every effort to charm the pretty young woman, holding doors open for her, pulling out chairs for her to sit, with nary a harsh word coming Kane's direction from anyone of the opposite sex.

The young man's brutal backhand, delivered as casually as one might slap at a bug, shocked Kane.S he felt shock to a degree that she'd never before felt in her life. For the first time in Kane's life, she realized that the normal rules of behavior didn't necessarily apply to everyone and that the large young man could and would hurt her without a second thought. For the first time in her life, Kane felt fear, real fear that flooded her entire being; fear and helplessness.

The young basketball player tossed his sobbing girlfriend aside, reached down, picked Kane up and began to shake her. Being just an inch or two under seven feet, he was able to hold Kane quite a distance up off of the ground as he cursed her loudly for her interference. Drunk, his Oklahoma born pale skin blotched red with anger, the young giant screamed obscenities and spittle in her face and Kane couldn't do anything about it, frozen like a rabbit trapped in the headlights of an oncoming car.

A couple of other college athletes, basketball buddies of the center summoned by his hysterical girlfriend, showed up and grabbed the young man, forcing him to drop Kane. She lay there, unable to move or even speak and dorm residents poured out of their rooms to watch as the jocks wrestled the young center to the ground and sat on him.

Finally Kane stood, went to her room and with shaking hands dialed nine-one-one. When the first policeman arrived on the scene, she was so relieved at the sight of him that she couldn't stop crying. Kane cried and her whole body shook like winter.

The star center received a reprimand from the Dean of Students and was benched for all of one game by his coach. Kane pushed for an expulsion and criminal charges but was stymied at every turn. No one in administration was willing to get radical with the player that may be taking the school to the NCAA championship.

None of the other students involved, including the abused girlfriend, would step up on her behalf, and without witnesses willing to come forward to testify. There was nothing to be done about criminal charges.

Whenever she saw the star basketball center on campus after that, he never failed to flash her a satisfied smile, a sneer that spoke, "I did it once and got away with it," the smile said silently to her, "and I could do it again whenever I want."

It was then that Emma Kane ceased being overly social with members of the opposite sex, in fact, stopped socializing with almost everyone.

A charming, outgoing young woman up until that point, she withdrew within herself, afraid of the cold spike of fear that pierced her chest whenever she was reminded of what happened that night. And she was reminded every single time she saw swaggering, muscular young men walking as though they owned the world. She saw them and she shook with fear.

Kane despised herself for the feeling and she despised those who caused her to feel that way. Her anger and fear grew to the extent that she knew that she absolutely had to do something or else it would destroy her. She chose to do two things. She signed up for a karate class on campus and she switched her major to law.

Her parents had not been pleased with the switch but consoled themselves that a career as a lawyer was almost as reputable as that of a doctor. What they didn't know was that their darling daughter never had any intention of going to law school, instead dreaming of a life in law enforcement. Unfortunately they never found out, either.

One afternoon during Kane's last semester of college, while driving home from the local grocery store, a drunk driver with a suspended license ran a stop sign and slammed into the Kane family station wagon, killing himself and both of Kane's parents.

A state trooper came to her dorm to deliver the sad news. Any lingering doubts about a career with a badge dissipated for good when she opened her dorm door to the man in uniform.

A year later, Kane found herself clad in her own uniform and driving the streets of Washington DC, a city with one of the highest crime rates in the country. Her very first week on the job began auspiciously. Kane and her partner responded to a disturbing the peace call from a local bar late one night. A large drunken man rampaged within the establishment, voicing his displeasure at being cut off by the bartender by tossing barstools through the plate glass windows of the front of the bar.

Her partner at that time was Brady, a muscular, over-bearing man who waited all of ten minutes before making a pass at Kane on her first day. She was pretty sure he was on steroids, but aside from the mistaken belief that he was God's gift to women, he was a pretty good cop and knew the street well. Together they confronted the rampaging drunk.

Brady, police baton in hand, first tried reasoning with the big man, which only resulted in a stool tossed in the direction of Brady's head. Brady dodged the stool, stepped in and swung his baton right for the man's skull. Though drunk, he wasn't slow, and the big man caught Brady's arm with the baton in mid-swing. The drunk picked up Brady by the belt and tossed him right over the bar with a crash. The barflies watching the show responded with cheers at the sight of a cop flying through the air.

Instinctively, Kane leaped to her partner's aid without a second thought. The big drunk swung a meaty fist in a vicious swipe at her face. Kane bobbed right under it, kicked the drunk in the crotch and when he howled in pain, hooked his left foot with her police baton and pulled, yanking his feet right out from under him. The big man hit the ground with a huge thud. When he next opened his eyes, the drunk found himself staring at Kane's pistol, drawn and pointed directly at his face.

"Don't move a fucking muscle," Kane said, her voice and aim steady as a rock.

Brady climbed back over the bar, blood dripping from a cut over his eyebrow, said, "Welcome to our nation's capital," and kicked the drunk in the floating ribs before rolling him over to cuff him.

"Good work, rookie," Brady said. "Are you having fun yet?"

Kane offered her partner a polite smile but inside, inside, she was grinning her ass off. She HAD had fun, but not for any reason Brady could have known. The fear that had been given birth to on that night in the dorm during her junior year, the cold shaking dread that had followed her for the past three years and had been her constant companion, it was gone. The fear was gone.

The fear would stay gone for the next ten years, in the face of many a sticky situation, both on patrol as a uniform and later as a detective in Homicide. Kane would do her job with great pride and skill, never suspecting that it would be any other way for her. Never believing it was possible to feel the fear as she had when she was a young girl.

Never knowing it would all change one day in a van on a highway. After The Van Incident, Kane's hands and heart shook no matter how she fought it.

CHAPTER 10

The other thing that Kane realized about herself was that she did not sit still very well. This wasn't actually new information. Kane had always known it about herself but always conveniently forgot about it until the next time she had to sit and twiddle her thumbs, be it on stakeout or flying a desk in an office.

Right now it was obvious that the locals were letting the feds stew in their own juice for a while. Kane flipped through the most recent forensic files on her desk, helpfully dropped off by a wide-eyed rookie cop who looked like he would be ready to shave any day now.

Thorne had taken charge of a large desk in one corner with a view of the map on the wall, plugged in a CD player and set up a travel chessboard. John Coltrane blared as Thorne considered the chessboard in front of him and moved one of the white pawns on the board. He still hadn't said much of anything about anything and it was beginning to irk Kane.

"Have you seen the latest forensic report from the Frederickson house?" Kane asked.

Thorne glanced up at Kane. He took the report from her, gave it a quick look and set it on the table next to his chessboard.

"So what do you think?" Kane asked.

"What do I think about what?"

"What do you think about the forensics report?"

"It's about what I expected," Thorne shrugged.

"Thorne," Kane said after a minute, clearly exasperated, "aren't you interested in it at all?"

"Not really, no."

"So you're not interested in catching this creep?"

"Forensics is not, in this particular case, how we're going catch this 'creep,'" Thorne moved a black pawn and turned the board around so that he could play the white side.

"How are we going to catch him?"

"By figuring out where he's going and beating or meeting him there."

"So where's he going?"

"If I already knew that, swivel-hips, would I be sitting here wasting my time talking to you?"

"York isn't far from here, maybe we should go take a look at the Frederickson house?" Kane asked.

"What for?"

"What for? To get a feel for it, get the picture of how our subject got in and out, see it with our own eyes. It's still a fresh scene."

"No."

"No? Why not?"

"Because it's not fresh, it was fresh the moment it was discovered and that moment has passed. Because timing is everything, Kane. And because I said so. Now go away and stop bothering me," Thorne made a move with a white pawn, turned the board around and considered the game from the black point of view.

"What are you doing?" Kane asked after a moment.

"I'm playing chess."

"Who are you playing?"

"Me. I'm playing me."

"You're playing with yourself?"

This comment earned Kane an ugly look from Thorne. She settled back into her chair and gazed up at the wall. The grade-school pictures of all the victims, posited next to what post-op photos there were to be had, chafed at her intestinal tract like nails on a chalkboard. Gilday and Scroggins approached.

"How long is Captain Asshole going to let us cool our heels here?" Kane demanded.

"Could be quite awhile, he is the captain, and he's probably paying you back for Riggs," Scroggins said. "Norm told us he was sending his guy over to brief you on the latest."

"In all fairness to Captain Asshole, that Riggs was a real piece of work, it was a nightmare, guy was totally out of his gourd," Gilday said.

"You ever work with Riggs?" Scroggins asked.

"Don't know him. Thorne?" Kane leaned forward in her chair.

"What?"

"Did you know Riggs?" she asked.

"I didn't know him, I knew of him."

"And?"

"Fuck up from Day One."

"How did he even get into ISU in the first place?" Kane asked.

"Same way you did, sweet-cakes. Affirmative Action." This comment earned Thorne a return ugly glare from Kane.

"Forsythe's got a couple of registered sex offenders he likes, but no hard evidence on anybody," Gilday said.

"Captain loves registered sex offenders, sounds really

good when he says it on television," Scroggins added. "Other than that, the sum total of who we like for this is jack fucking shit."

"Jesus Christ, over twenty kids and there's nothing?" Kane shook her head.

"Look, I don't want you to think we're not taking this serious," Gilday said. "Believe me when I say that we're pissed off and busting our asses here."

"And there has been a fucking parade of people coming to Nebraska to try and tell us how to do our job," Scroggins said. "We've had independent profilers, psychologists, psychics, investigative reporters from both print and television who want solve this before we do and none of them have done anything other than slow us down. We even had some dumb shit, this plumber who was working on a book, he used his own daughter as bait to try and catch the Iceman and get rich off of it."

"We busted him on child endangerment laws and now his ex-wife has sole custody," Gilday said. "You name the fruit-cake, we've gotten it.

"I mean, Captain Asshole is an asshole, make no mistake about that," he continued. "And he likes reporters. But he's covering all the bases, crossing his t's and dotting his i's, he's doing what he's supposed to be doing. If he wasn't, he would have been gone by now."

"We got over a hundred men working this from every angle all over the state, forensics teams double-checking each other and uniforms knocking on every door there is. We're doing everything that we can do. That's one of the reasons Jeff and I are here," Scroggins said.

"Our boss wants us to make sure that everything that can be done is done to catch this killer, but this guy is a fucking ghost," Gilday said.

"It's like he can walk through walls without leaving evidence," Scroggins added.

"There's a lot of resentment against the feds by the folks around here right now," Gilday said. "Part of it is that fuck-up Riggs that was here first, and part of it is the fact this Mercy Killer is running around the country killing everybody, we're all watching it on television and you all haven't done a damn thing about it."

This got Thorne's attention and he perked up, leveling an even gaze at Gilday.

"But as far as Gerry and me are concerned, and everyone working here, we only want this fucker caught, we don't care how it's done," Gilday continued. "If it's you guys or Captain Asshole or Spider-Man who does it, we don't care. We want to catch him. If you can help us, we're with you. If you can't, then stay out of the way. That's what it comes down to."

"Pretty much. So what do you think, Thorne?" Scroggins asked.

"About what?"

"Can you help us with the Iceman?" Gilday asked.

"Eventually."

Thorne returned to his solo chess game. Gilday and Scroggins waited for him to elaborate but he didn't and this confused them. They looked to Kane for help but she didn't have anything more to offer either. Scroggins and Gilday glanced at each other and shook their heads in unison, pretty sure that they had another federal cuckoo on their hands.

CHAPTER 11

Betty shoveled snow from her driveway while keeping an eye on her eight year-old daughter Janis as she played in the snow with the family dog, a chocolate Labrador named Pooh. Pooh was named by Janis after the famous Disney bear, though the name took on an added dimension as Pooh the Labrador demonstrated, at an early age, an amazing ability to produce prodigious amounts of excrement almost at will. Betty's husband never failed to see the humor in that, though he rarely had to clean up after the damn dog.

Betty stopped and wiped her brow, as always a little unnerved by the wooded area located next to her house. At night it always seemed dark and creepy, despite the many yard lights her husband put up at her insistence.

She probably shouldn't let Janis out here past dark, but the young girl loved being outside when the snow was falling in big fat flakes, and besides, Betty liked to stay ahead of the shoveling before it got too high in the driveway. If she left it up to her husband, he would just let it pile up and drive his truck right through it.

Today, for some reason, the dark woods spooked Betty more than usual. She decided that she'd done enough for the night. Pooh barked happily as Janis laughed and tossed snow in the air.

"Okay Janis, time to go in, it's almost supper time."

"No!"

"Don't give me any lip, young lady, let's go. Your dad's going to be home from work soon and I want your bath done before he gets here."

"Five more minutes!"

"In the house, now!"

Betty hefted her shovel over her shoulder and walked up her driveway into her garage. It was a bit cramped with all their junk plus her car parked in there, a mess as always. Pooh barked, louder than usual.

Hasn't that girl gone in yet, Betty thought with a frown, she'd better not make me chase her all around the yard or there will be hell to pay. Stepping around the bumper of her car, Betty bumped into a large bag of road salt and spilled it all over the garage floor.

"Shit," Betty cursed under her breath, kneeled down and tried unsuccessfully to scoop some of the road salt back into the bag. The barking of the dog rose to a fever pitch and then stopped with a yelp.

Betty froze and listened closely. She heard nothing, nothing at all, and that chilled her more than the ice and snow ever could.

"Janis? Janis!" Betty jumped up and hurried out of the garage, heart suddenly in her mouth. She ran quickly down her driveway. Janis was nowhere in sight. Pooh the Labrador lay unmoving on its side in the yard, a pillow of red snow cushioning its head. Betty ran toward the dead dog, looking around at the woods next to her home, and the county road running by her house, into the night and snow surrounding her, beyond frantic now.

"Janis! JANIS!"

Betty ran for the woods, stumbling through the snow, screaming Janis's name over and over.

CHAPTER 12

The local profiler's name was Simms, which immediately reminded Kane of the video game by the same name, the one where you can simulate life-forms and interactive social systems on a computer, be they animal or human. She'd played that game on her home computer while on leave after The Van Incident.

Simms didn't come across as terribly interactive himself. A pale older detective who had unfortunately given in to the aging man's impulse to comb-over the bare spots on his scalp, Simms would compulsively reach up and pat his hair to make sure it was in place as he briefed them. His suit was shiny with age and Simms wore suspenders instead of a belt, along with a rather ratty tie.

Kane also noticed he didn't look them in the eye or offer to shake hands, just said his name was Simms and that he was going to try to bring them up to date. His voice was higher than she would have thought, it had a flat nasality that reminded Kane of a social studies teacher she'd had in junior high.

Gilday and Scroggins had decided earlier that they would

join in on the briefing, each man telling himself that it was in the best interest of the case at hand to quickly orientate the feds and that it had nothing at all to do with the slope of Kane's cheek or the firmness of her grip.

It was already late, after eight-thirty, the delay in Simms's briefing yet another indication of the low regard held for them by the locals. For a moment Kane thought that Thorne wasn't even going to sit in and listen to what Simms had to say. When Thorne noticed everyone looking at him, he calmly leaned back away from his chessboard, crossed his arms and waited for Simms to begin.

"I know that you've read through the files so I'll just hit the highlights," Simms began. "We have twenty-three victims counting Wendy Frederickson, the young girl abducted last night in York. Ages range from five to twelve, twenty of the girls were Caucasian, two Asian and one African-American. We've run the MO through VICAP to see if there were any cases similar in other states but so far there aren't.

"The first victim that we know of was five year-old Katherine Fitzgerald. She was abducted in North Platte thirteen months ago by our UNSUB in the middle of the day from her own house. He was seen by the vic's brother, who was fourteen at the time and babysitting. The brother came out of the kitchen with snacks for the two of them and there the guy is. Our UNSUB sapped the boy on the head and disappeared with the girl. Description of our perp was a tall man, dressed in black and wearing a black ski mask, similar to what the Fredericksons remember. The house was locked, both before and after. The body of the girl was never found," Simms said as he reached up to check his hair.

"He's been spotted in seven of the abductions and the description is always the same, though sometimes witnesses vary the height and weight."

"We think he likes being seen," Gilday said.

"He probably gets off on it," Scroggins added.

"It's likely there was no need in the first disappearance to sap the brother, he was in the kitchen for a substantial amount of time," Simms actually looked grateful for the troopers' interruption. "Our USUB had significant opportunity to abduct the girl without encountering anyone. We think he waited for the kid purposefully.

"Same holds true with last night's abduction. He's subdued parents and or babysitters with a sap three times and a stun gun four, including last night," Simms continued. "He's taken them from their homes, from church, from bathrooms at malls, outside in their parents' cars, and once at a pediatrician's office. We have fibers and footprints in several instances but so far nothing conclusive.

"We've recovered remains of only nine of our missing children, victims three, seven, eight, twelve through fifteen, nineteen and twenty-one. We've never recovered a body whole, usually we only get parts, so our guy is probably keeping trophies. Victims thirteen, fifteen, nineteen and twenty-one were left the most intact, with torsos and heads. He may have been interrupted at work in those situations."

Kane wasn't new to this sort of talk, but still she felt bile rise up to the back of her throat. It affected Scroggins and Gilday as well; she could feel the visible anger from the troopers as they listened to Simms recount the details. Thorne just stared impassively.

"He's using a blade with a serrated edge, but never the same one, to part his vics out; that coupled with his choice of prey and appearance are the only signs of consistency he's demonstrated. The consensus is that our subject is not a newbie at this, he's too clean and bold. That's what we know so far."

"What don't we know?" Kane asked. Thorne glanced at her and for a moment she thought the look in his eye was one of approval, but the moment passed quickly. Simms cleared his throat.

"Unfortunately, there's a lot that we don't know," Simms replied. "We don't know how long he keeps them alive before killing them. We don't know what he does to them when he has them, we don't have any evidence of rape so far, we don't know where he keeps them when he takes them or where they're killed when they get killed.

"We don't know how he chooses the girls he chooses or why. His incubation periods have no consistency, those that we're aware of. Sometimes body parts show up a couple of days later, sometimes a couple of weeks. Sometimes they don't. All we really know is he takes little girls and kills them. That's it.

"We think we're dealing with a trapdoor spider personality here, someone with a house with some privacy and probably a big basement. Given the ease with which he's handled alarms and locks, we also think that it's likely he works as a locksmith or for an alarm installation company, if not at this point then sometime earlier in his life.

"He's probably self-employed now, which gives him freedom in terms of time and schedule, and he owns a panel van. He's probably a sexual offender, most likely has a history of such offenses from an early age and he has trouble adjusting socially even to this day."

Simms coughed and patted his comb-over again. "Any questions?"

"What's that on your hip, is that a forty-four?" Thorne gestured toward the weapon just visible under Simms's jacket. "Looks like a Taurus forty-four Mag."

"Uh, yes," Simms replied and instinctively touched his gun, reassuring himself that it was still there.

"That's one hell of a revolver. Handy if you think you're going to run into any rhinos."

"It's a stopper," Simms said.

"Do you know what you smell like to me, Mr. Simms, with your squeaky voice, cheap shoes and oversized elephant gun? You reek of inadequacy."

Simms flushed and allowed himself a quick glance at Kane.

"What?"

"I said you reek of inadequacy, that's what I said. You smell. Let me guess. Grew up watching Hawaii Five-O, didn't you? Dreamed of someday being like Steve McGarrett, catch criminals and kiss girls in grass skirts, is that it?"

"Listen …" Simms stuttered.

"Only thing is, you live in cow country, you're not quite tall enough, your jaw isn't square, your voice isn't deep as Jack Lord's and you look like a fucking librarian. Everyone is always surprised to find out you carry a badge because you don't look or sound like a cop at all and there's a part of you that believes maybe everyone's right, maybe you shouldn't be wearing one, maybe you don't have what it takes to be a badge. So you drift into forensics where among the lab rats and techs you kind of fit in but you still wonder about yourself, don't you?"

"Hey," Scroggins, who had been listening open-mouthed, snapped out of his shock. Simms was lock-jawed and a stunning shade of purple.

"And that, Mr. Simms, that is the foul source of inadequacy. You're so caught up in who and what you AREN'T that you're NOT properly doing your job. You're just filling out the forms, 'crossing the t's and dotting the i's,' collecting a paycheck and not doing anything about what's happening here. You're missing the obvious."

"Hey, Thorne," Scroggins objected.

"Hey what?"

"Maybe you're forgetting that you're a guest here, you know?" Scroggins's color was also up.

"Guest? I'm not a fucking guest, sport, what do you think this is, a bed and breakfast? I'm here to fix this problem."

"What problem, the problem caused by the last fibbie that was sent here? Riggs-"

"I don't want to hear another goddamn word about Riggs," Thorne said. "Riggs was probably the best thing to happen to you all here because he gave you a convenient excuse."

"You know what? Fuck you," Gilday said. "All of us, Simms and the two of us and everyone in this building, we've been busting our butts for a year here and if there was any possible way to catch the Iceman up to this point then we would have done it by now, so fuck you."

"You're right about the Iceman but I'm not talking about the Iceman, I'm talking about the other guy."

"Other guy, what other guy?" Scroggins asked.

"The other guy," Thorne unwrapped a fresh stick of gum.

Scroggins and Gilday looked at each other, confused. Simms struggled to move his mouth and get his normal pale color back. Kane tried to think of something to say but was at a loss for the moment.

"You do know that there's two of them killing kids in your state, right?" Thorne asked after getting his gum going.

"Two serial killers?" Simms asked, finally finding his voice.

"Yes."

"Two serial killers?" Simms asked again.

"Absolutely."

"Two guys working together?" Scroggins asked.

"Two guys yes, working together no. You have two separate serial killers here."

"How do you know?" Kane asked.

"It's right in front of you, all you had to do is read the fucking report. Four kills belong to somebody other than the Iceman. In other words, you have a copycat."

"But ..." Simms was back to stuttering.

Thorne stood and went to the map on the wall, using it to illustrate his points.

"Look at victims thirteen, fifteen, nineteen and twenty-one, the four bodies that when discovered were the most intact. There was a reason for that, you fucking wanna-be. Look at how close these four kills are, they are close in time and more importantly close in distance; that's not happened in any other abduction.

"Those four abduction-murders occurred in a thirty-mile radius of this town called Brainard, which sits right in the exact center of all four kills. That's killer number two, your copycat. This guy lives in this area, he's been following the papers and staging his kills so they look like the Iceman's."

"Holy shit," Scroggins said.

"Oh my God," Simms whispered to himself.

"He's put some time into making his kills look like Iceman's but he's not as smart as he thinks he is; there's a world of differences between his kills and Iceman's. First of all, the Iceman has never hit the same town more than once so far, so why would he start with the Brainard area? Second, the Iceman started west and is moving east in a slow but steady path mostly along the interstate.

"Except for Brainard, which is much farther north than any of his other kills and too far to the west, it would mean that the Iceman is backtracking and I don't see him doing that. Third, look at each of the four Brainard area abductions.

"First girl was snatched out of her dad's car at a gas station while Dad was inside paying for gas. It was nine-thirty at night, how did our guy know Dad was going to stop for gas at that gas station? How did he know Dad was going to pay cash and not charge it? He didn't, he just happened to be there by chance and snatched the girl while Dad's back was turned and made off with her. They found the body the next morning. The Iceman would never do that. Shortest discovery time for the Iceman is six days.

"Traffic going back and forth, it's a busy intersection. Lucky nobody saw him. It wasn't a careful grab. Crime of opportunity, the Iceman would never do that. All four of these snatches were opportunistic, and each of the four bodies was discovered in less than seventy-two hours. They were not the work of the Iceman, he's a control freak, he would never do that. This guy is sloppier, most of the evidence you have is from him, he's practically left you road signs and you should have fucking caught him by now. The Iceman is a smart crafty fucker and he's going to be a bitch to catch, but this guy is somebody different and it should have been obvious to you the minute he popped up."

Kane regarded Thorne with newfound respect. Gilday and Scroggins glanced at Simms, who has again flushed and had for once forgotten about his hair.

"I can see it. Makes sense, Jeff," Scroggins said to Gilday.

"Yeah. What do you think, Ken?" Gilday asked Simms gently. Simms took a deep breath and exhaled.

"I'll have to, uh, run it by the team, and the captain, of course," Simms coughed and fidgeted. "But I guess that it's definitely possible and if true, it would explain some things. He could be right."

"You guess? If true? Could be right? What kind of chickenshit outfit is this, anyway?"

"Hold on a minute, Thorne," Gilday said. "With all due respect, you've been here all of six hours and we don't know each other very well yet, so forgive us for not dropping our drawers immediately for a short-arm inspection from you, okay?"

"Look, stud-"

"Could you please stop this aggressive male posturing, all of you? It's not getting us anywhere," Kane said. "What can we do now?"

"I'm going to get back to the team and fly the theory by them, see what they think and if they clear it we'll update the captain," Simms said as he gathered up some of his materials. "We'll do up an analysis, post it on the hotline and of course CC you on it."

"Two serial killers, shit," Scroggins said. "What if Thorne's right, Jeff?"

"What if I'm right? Simms!" Thorne snapped his fingers.

Simms, who'd already begun his hasty retreat, stopped and turned toward Thorne.

"What?"

"Let me ask you a question. Where did they get the title for the show Hawaii Five-O?"

"They ... uh, called the show that because Hawaii is the fiftieth state."

"Here's a more difficult one. What was Jack Lord's real name?"

Simms coughed and stared at the floor for a moment before answering.

"The name on Jack Lord's birth certificate was John Joseph Patrick Ryan," Simms replied.

Thorne looked at Kane and the troopers triumphantly.

"What if I'm right? Of course I'm right."

Simms's reluctant demonstration of TV trivia was interrupted by the entrance of Forsythe and Hairston into headquarters, fresh from their latest press briefing. Forsythe shrugged off his winter jacket and stamped over to Kane and Thorne's cubicle.

"All right," Forsythe said as he loosened his tie. "Do you two have anything to offer me besides the usual bullshit?"

Thorne looked at Forsythe, composing in his mind a truly sarcastic comment, but before Thorne could unleash it, one of the uniforms, a young sergeant named Johnson, stood and waved for Forsythe's attention.

"Captain, it's Reilly, he says it's a priority!" Johnson ran to Forsythe and handed him a phone.

"Forsythe," Forsythe barked into the phone. He listened for a minute. "Are you sure, are you absolutely fucking sure? Good. Sit tight, you'll be hearing from us."

Forsythe tossed the phone back to Johnson, stood up on a chair and whistled to get the attention of everyone on the floor. Heads popped up from cubicles everywhere.

"All right, everyone, we just had the break we were waiting for! That was the lab. They got something on the body parts found in Central City, the remains of the Moeller girl. They found a pubic hair belonging to an African-American male!"

An excited murmur went through the room. Forsythe swiveled to Hairston.

"Norm, who was that black guy we liked in Kearney?"

"Carl Mitchell, convicted sex offender," Hairston replied. "He's the only African-American we looked at, a part-time truck driver, no alibis for many if not most of the abductions. We interviewed but he lawyered up and we had nothing solid to hold him on."

"Now we do. Get on the horn, I want him picked up pronto, I want warrants for his house and DNA sampling, I want it matched with the hair we found and I want him in the box and spilling his skeevy guts out! Let's go!"

Forsythe jumped down and grabbed his jacket as everyone in the room started moving all at once.

"You're making a mistake," Thorne said as he casually made another move on his chessboard.

"What was that?" Forsythe practically skidded to a stop.

"I said, you're making a mistake, he's not your guy."

"How do you know?" Scroggins asked.

"The Iceman is white, not black. No black man had anything to do with this."

"Oh shit, here we go again!" Forsythe slammed his jacket down. "What is it with you fucking feds, anyway? Why do you always think that it's a white guy doing the serial killing?"

"Primarily because the men we have been catching at it always seem to be white," Thorne retorted. "Not only that, I've been here all day and I haven't even seen a dark-haired person, much less a dark-skinned one. How many black people do you even have in this state, anyway?"

"Two point eight percent of the total population," Kane offered, grateful for her earlier research.

"Two point eight percent? You want to tell me that in a state with less than three percent black people in it, a black man is somehow going to be able drop into different small towns where everyone is white as Casper the fucking Ghost, waltz in and waltz out with a young white girl under his arm and NO ONE, not a neighbor, not a gas station attendant, not one person reports a stranger with a dark face? Come on."

"We have a goddamn pubic hair from a black man!"

"I don't doubt that you do, but said pubic hair did not come from the nether regions of the Iceman. There will be some other explanation."

"I can't believe I'm going through this fucking bullshit again," Forsythe pointed his finger at Thorne. "Look, Slick, I remember this guy Mitchell, I sweated him on the box when we first brought him in four months ago, he's guilty, I don't care what color he is, he's guilty, I could smell it on him. As far as I'm concerned, we've got our killer in our sights," Forsythe picked up his coat again.

"Which one?" Thorne asked.

"What?" Forsythe stopped.

"Which killer do you have in your sights?"

"What the fuck ..."

"Uh, Captain," Simms found his voice again, "Agent Thorne has reason to believe that we are dealing with two subjects here."

"What? What is this happy horseshit?"

"Agent Thorne believes ..."

"You have two separate serial killers at work here. One of the jokers is masking his kills to make them look like the first one, but you definitely got two here," Thorne said. "And neither of them is black."

"I don't believe this! Are you deliberately trying to fuck me up on this?" Forsythe was incredulous. "Was that why you were sent here, to deliberately fuck up this investigation like the other guy did? I don't have time to fuck around with you, the Frederickson girl might still be alive and you're here dicking me around! You! Stay out of my way, understand? Let's go, Norm, I want to be there when they slap the bracelets on Mitchell. Goddamn fucking feds!"

Forsythe put on his jacket and stormed off, Hairston close on his heels. Scroggins, Gilday and Kane looked at Thorne. Simms turned a darker shade of purple and snuck off with his reports. Everyone else in the large room suddenly found something better to do elsewhere, away from Thorne.

"Well, I have to say," Gilday said, "you sure are making friends fast here."

"I'm not here to whisper sweet nothings and hand out hand-jobs, fellas. I'm here to tell you what I know, whether you like it or not."

"I think you're right about there being two killers," Scroggins said, "but are you sure neither of them is black?"

"I wouldn't say so if I wasn't; both of these killers are white."

"The DC snipers were black," Gilday pointed out.

"I wouldn't classify them as serial killers," Thorne said.

"What the hell else would you call them?" Scroggins exclaimed.

"Technically, I would call them spree killers. They just happened to be a little more careful than most. Careful spree killers, it's a new category. They were spree killers, the Iceman is a serial killer."

"What's the difference?" Scroggins asked.

"Kane?" Thorne put her on the spot.

"In spree killing, the identity of the victims is secondary and oftentimes incidental to the act," Kane recited. "Once they decide to go, spree killers kill who's available, which we have seen at post offices and schools, acting in response to their anger at something beyond the individual victims in their path. For serial killers, the victims and what they represent to the killer are primary to the act, almost as if they have a relationship that's personal."

Kane caught another glimmer of approval from Thorne.

"Yeah, but Thorne," Gilday said, "what difference does all that make now? We got evidence now, we got to follow the evidence to where it leads us and if it leads us to a black man, then that's all she wrote."

Johnson popped up again, holding a phone to his ear.

"Hey, Jeff, is the captain gone?" Johnson asked. "I got another priority."

"He's probably already on his way to Kearney, Bill, what's up?"

"He's already in the transit, Rich, call Norm on his phone,"

Johnson said into the phone. "Did you post it? He's online on the mobile in the truck."

"What's up, Bill?" Scroggins asked after Johnson hung up.

"There's just been another abduction, three miles outside of Brainard," Johnson said, hesitant. "Reilly's posting it on the hotline right now and we're putting her out as an Amber Alert. She was snatched not even ten minutes ago."

"Bingo, there's our copycat again, what'd I tell you?" Thorne said.

Kane immediately refreshed the hotline on her desktop computer and hit print.

"Shit, that was quick too," Scroggins said. "It's not far away, Jeff, let's follow CSU over to the abduction site, get a look at it ourselves, what do you say?"

"Affirmative on that, buddy."

"Kane," Thorne said, "do you remember what I said about timing?"

"Of course. Timing is everything."

"Guess what, time is here and now," Thorne pointed his finger at Johnson. "You, what's your name?"

"Sergeant Johnson."

"Johnson, I need a car," Thorne grabbed his coat.

"We're going?" Kane asked.

"You're going?" Scroggins asked.

"Hell yes, this scene is red hot and I want a whiff. Johnson, get me a car."

"Uh, the captain said …"

"I don't care what the captain said, Johnson, get me some fucking transportation!" Thorne snapped. Johnson looked to the troopers for help. Technically, he'd been assigned to the troopers by Forsythe to act as their assistant so it was their call, but most everyone walked in fear of offending the captain, and helping the fibbies was one definite way of doing it.

"Come on, Bill," Gilday said. "It won't hurt if they take a look with us. We'll all go together. We can follow up with CSU while the captain deals with Mitchell. Get some keys and we'll get going."

Thorne put on his coat and made one more move on his chessboard. He checked his weapon and walked off without looking behind him.

"Let's rock and roll, kids," Thorne rubbed his hands together and Kane would swear that he was almost gleeful at the prospect of what lay ahead.

CHAPTER 13

Bill Johnson nervously guided a police van through the dark county roads of Nebraska on the way to Brainard, Gilday, Scroggins, Kane and Thorne in the back.

"Janis Jacobson, eight years old," Kane read out loud from the printed report. "Playing in her front yard with her dog. Mother turns her back for a moment, girl is gone and the dog is dead."

"Crime of opportunity," Scroggins said.

"Dog was stabbed, right?" Thorne asked.

"Throat cut."

"The Iceman never killed any dogs," observed Gilday.

"This guy isn't him by a long shot. Biggest difference between this guy and the Iceman is how this guy leaves the bodies. His cuts are more jagged and rushed. He's obviously stimulated by the kill and gets a little messy despite himself. If the Iceman is messy, he doesn't let us see it.

"With this guy's other four homicides, you found the body within forty-eight hours. He's impatient as hell and that means this one will turn up soon and not far from where she was abducted," Thorne said. "He parts them out, but not nearly to the extent that the Iceman does. You've found most of the parts buried not far from the bodies on these four. Never happens with the Iceman, when you find part of a body, that's the only part you ever get. You never recover anything else after the initial discovery. Most of the Iceman's vics you never recover. You've gotten every Brainard girl.

"Two more major differences," Thorne continued. "First one is the panties. This guy loves to play with the panties, once they were tied to a tree nearby, once stuffed in her mouth; he likes to be funny with the panties. Iceman doesn't do that. Second major difference is that Mr. FunnyPants doesn't like to be watched. He covered the eyes of his victims with something, all four times. He has to. That's his signature."

"Jesus Christ, why didn't somebody say something before this?" Scroggins asked.

"Why didn't you notice it, sport?" Thorne asked.

"Hey ..."

"You're right," Gilday interrupted Scroggins before he could get going, "we should have caught that. What else do you got?"

"This guy, FunnyPants, he lives in the area. You've probably interviewed and looked at him already. He's white, eighteen to twenty-five, unemployed high school dropout. History of depression and probable suicide attempts, he's been in a mental institution at least once and currently taking prescription medication. No driver's license, probably lives with a single relative who looks after him. I would say he has a deformity on his face, a cleft lip or a scar, something significant that draws negative attention."

Scroggins and Gilday looked at each other.

"Holy shit," Scroggins said under his breath, "that sounds like ..."

"Someone you know?" Thorne asked.

Scroggins's cell phone rang and he answered it.

"Yeah," Gilday replied, "someone we looked hard at. He had a rock-solid alibi, though."

"What? No shit?" Scroggins exclaimed.

"What is it?" Thorne asked.

"They found the Jacobson girl's body already," Scroggins hung up the phone, "right outside of Garrison."

"That was fast," Kane said.

"Fastest recovery yet, this one is nuclear-hot," Scroggins said.

"Garrison is only five or six miles from Brainard," Gilday said.

"Then that's where we go first," Thorne said. "Johnson! We're going to Garrison and stop riding the brake; we want to get there sometime tonight."

Kane noticed that the dynamic had shifted and there was no doubt as to who was in charge now. She found that interesting, to say the least.

CHAPTER 14

I n a cornfield a mile outside of Garrison, searchlights lit up the sky and a tarp covered the dumpsite to protect it from the heavy snowfall. Uniformed men and vehicles surround the site and cordoned off the area with police tape. A forensics team took photos and searched thoroughly for trace evidence as Scroggins and Gilday observed. Kane viewed the body for a long moment before rejoining Thorne, standing off by himself away the group.

"Are you going to take a look?" Kane asked him.

"Nope."

"Why not?'

"I'm looking at other things."

"How could somebody do that to a child?" Kane asked, looking ill.

"HOW is easy," Thorne replied. "HOW is always easy. Why, why is what's important."

"Then why, fucking why?"

"Why do you think?"

Kane thought on that, realizing that Thorne was again testing her.

"He's angry."

"Who isn't angry? We're all angry, Kane."

Kane caught the disdain in his voice and it cut her. She struggled to think but images of the dead child cluttered her mind. Gilday joined them.

"Throat cut, perp was standing behind her when he did it. Flesh cut off from the back, buttocks and legs, similar to the Iceman. Arm and foot missing."

"But she wasn't killed here," Thorne stated.

"No," Gilday admitted. "No spray. She was killed somewhere else and left here."

"Time of death?"

"Rough estimate till they get her on the table, but they're saying hour or two, tops. Not long at all. We got lucky, one of the town cops out looking for her spotted the body. Quickest recovery time yet and there's a lot of trace left at this one that they were able to get to before the weather did."

"Panties?"

"Panties tied around her head, covering her eyes," Kane answered for Gilday.

"Hello, Mr. FunnyPants," Thorne walked around and looked at the dark empty Nebraska fields and farmland surrounding him. "Why here, why did the body end up here?"

"You all right?' Gilday asked Kane.

"No. I'm pretty fucking far from all right," she answered.

"He doesn't drive, he didn't walk. Why here? Can't tell what kind of tracks he left because the falling snow," Thorne continued. "Does it ever stop snowing in this shithole?"

Scroggins joined them. "Jesus Christ, every time I have to look at one of these it burns my ass. You puke again, Jeff?"

"No, shut up."

"He always pukes whenever we have to look at bodies," Scroggins said. "Are you holding it in?"

"No, shut up, dickhead."

"What? It's not like I blame you," Scroggins replied.

"Wake up, kids," Thorne interrupted. "What's that over there?"

They all looked in the direction Thorne pointed to, off in the darkness. By the shadows cast from the spotlights, an extremely large building could be seen just on the edge of town, about a half a mile away.

"Grain silo," Scroggins said.

"A what?" Thorne asked.

"A grain silo," Kane said.

Thorne started walking toward the grain silo. Everyone reluctantly followed him.

"Okay. What the hell is a grain silo?" Thorne asked, wading through the snow. Everyone hurried to catch up to him.

"A grain silo is where they store grain. Grain is harvested all fall, stored here most of the winter until it's sold. Sometimes it's called a grain elevator, that's what we called it," Gilday said, "grain elevator."

They all trudged along silently for a bit, the flashing lights and sirens fading in the distance. Thorne reached the foot of the grain silo and stopped, staring up at it. It was a large, round, cement building, rising up almost three hundred feet in the air. A dark forbidding granite presence that stood large in the night. Kane felt small before it.

"Big bastard, isn't it? I've been seeing these buildings all over the place and wondered what they were."

"You're in Nebraska, Thorne," Kane said, snippy. "That's what they do here. That's why they have all those things called farms that we saw when we flew over. What are you doing?"

"I'm seeing the sights, this is my first time in Nebraska," Thorne pointed to a ladder going up the side of it. "You climb that ladder, all the way to the top, you could see for miles, right?"

"Well, I wouldn't do it when it was this cold and icy," Scroggins replied. "But yeah, you could."

"And who gives a shit?" Kane said. "What are we going to do now?"

"What's your problem?" Thorne asked.

"My problem?"

"Your time of the month, is that the problem? You riding the cotton pony this week or what?" he asked.

"Fuck you, Thorne, I tend to get a little cranky whenever a little girl gets killed!"

Gilday and Scroggins looked at each other, uncomfortable. Thorne was untouched by her outburst.

"You want to know what's really interesting?" Thorne asked after a moment.

"What?" Gilday asked.

"That," Thorne pointed his finger. "What's that there?"

They all turned and looked in the direction he was pointing. About twenty feet away, mostly hidden from view, was a steel trapdoor not far from the foot of the silo.

"That goes under the silo, to the gallery," Scroggins said.

"Gallery?" Thorne asked.

"Gallery, it's uh," Scroggins fumbled, "it's like a network of support tunnels underneath the silo."

"I never knew they were called that," Gilday said. We just called them the tunnels."

"I spent a summer working on silos in high school," Scroggins said. "I know a lot more about them than I'd like to."

Thorne threw the steel trapdoor open all the way and descended the ladder to the depths below.

"Well, you know what they say," Thorne winked at Scroggins before he disappeared into the dark.

"What's that?"

"Knowledge is power, young Jedi," Thorne said.

CHAPTER 15

At the foot of the ladder, down inside the gallery, everyone turned their flashlights on and splashed the light around. The cement walls were pitted and covered with obscene graffiti. Old empty beer cans and cigarette butts littered the floor. The tunnels seemed to go on and on into the ground. Thorne almost slipped on the snow under the ladder, catching himself just in time.

"Fuck! This fucking snow."

"You better get some good snow boots," Gilday said, "otherwise you're going to be sliding all over the place."

"I am not planning on being here long enough to need snow boots."

"How far does it go?" Kane asked as she walked down the tunnel, disappearing into the shadows.

"If it's like the others, a long ways, most are like a maze, with different stairs and levels, bunch of exits," Scroggins said.

"That trapdoor up there, it's never padlocked?" Thorne asked.

"Can't, fire code or something," Scroggins answered.

"Kids come down here all the time to, you know, drink or make out, least we did in our town."

"Bunch of us used to go down and play Dungeons and Dragons in the tunnels underneath our elevator when we were kids," Gilday said.

"Yeah, D & D, that and Empire Strikes Back, remember that, Jeff?" Scroggins added. "That was fun."

"So what, you two were geeks, is that what you're saying?" Thorne asked. "I had you pegged as jocks."

"A little bit of both, I guess," Gilday said.

"You think Mr. FunnyPants came in here?" Scroggins asked.

"I think this is his kind of place," Thorne answered. "Every town has a building, a silo, like this?"

"Big ones like this, yeah, some have more than one. There are smaller silos on some farms, but they don't usually have the gallery underneath," Scroggins said.

"Do you want to take a look farther down?" Kane asked.

"Go ahead, Kane, knock yourself out."

Kane slit her eyes at him and investigated farther down the tunnel.

"Who's this guy that you know, the one that fits the FunnyPants profile?" Thorne asked.

"Kid by the name of Ryan Robertson, twenty-two, lives with his grandma right outside of Brainard. Fits your profile to a T. Unemployed, doesn't drive, mental, everything. And the face?" Gilday said.

"Kid has really bad acne, I mean his face is a pizza with the works, anchovies, the whole deal," Scroggins added. "But his alibi was rock-solid, I'm telling you."

"Doesn't matter," Thorne sniffed, "he fits the profile, he's the one."

"But ..." Gilday said.

"Thorne!" Kane called from the darkness farther down the tunnel. "Thorne, get over here!"

Scroggins and Gilday ran to where Kane was crouched at an intersection of the tunnel. A small bloody snowsuit lay torn on the hard floor and silenced the Troopers. Kane played her flashlight on the wall of the tunnel. The wall was covered in blood.

"That's spray," she said simply. "We've found our kill spot."

Thorne, joining them, glanced at it and caught Gilday's eye.

"Call CSU, get them down here and started on processing this evidence," Thorne said, "and then call Johnson, tell him to get his head out of his ass and fire up the van, we gotta full-tilt boogie out of here right now. We don't have much time. I'm betting he stayed to watch us work the dumpsite and took off when we headed this way. He's probably heading home now and I want to beat him there."

"What?" Kane stood. "Where are we going?"

"We're going to see Mr. FunnyPants."

CHAPTER 16

Johnson unhappily guided the police van down the county roads once again with everyone loaded in the back. Kane made Johnson a little bit nervous, because of how Kane looked, and Thorne made Johnson a whole lot nervous, because of how Thorne looked at him. As a result, Johnson drove a little cautiously, which in turn caused Thorne a great deal of impatience. Thorne slapped the back of the driver's seat.

"Let's go, Johnson, I thought all you country boys could drive like hell!"

"I was born and raised in Lincoln," Johnson protested.

"What's that supposed to mean?"

"It means, I mean, it's not … it's a city, I'm not from the country."

"You live in Nebraska, Johnson, wake up and smell the cowshit. Let's go, move it!" Thorne slapped the back of the seat again.

"Do you have a file on this guy?" Kane asked Gilday.

"Yeah, but not with us, it's back at HQ. We liked this guy

Robertson a lot, but he's from Seattle and he's only been in this state for three months."

"Which is the window for the FunnyPants killings," Kane pointed out.

"Right, but we didn't know then that there were two killers, the Iceman had been going for months by then and Forsythe was pushing for the whole thing," Gilday said. "But the big stopping block is Robertson's alibi.

"He's an in-patient at Brainard Memorial Hospital, being treated for depression. Mental wing of the hospital, it's locked up so no one can get in or out without signing. He checks in every night at seven, out every morning at seven. All of the Brainard area abductions were after seven at night, just like this last one, and the staff confirmed he's been there every night since he moved here."

Scroggins hung up his cell phone.

"Okay, Grandma Robertson dropped him off at quarter to seven like she always does. Hospital said he signed in and was there for lights out. They just looked in on him and confirmed that he's there now.

"Bullshit, we have to see for ourselves," Thorne snorted.

"What?" Scroggins said. "But they said ..."

"I don't care what THEY said, he fits the profile, he's the one. Brainard Hospital, Johnson, we don't have much time so stop lagging," Thorne thumped the back of the seat again.

"What the hell, Gerry," Gilday said. "Won't hurt to look."

"Fuck it, yeah," Scroggins said. "If Thorne's wrong at least then we can give him shit about it."

"Listen boys, it works like this," Thorne said. "I am ALWAYS right. Learn it, know it and live it."

"He's modest, too," added Kane.

Johnson nervously cleared his throat. "Shouldn't we call Captain Forsythe?"

"What for?" Thorne said.

"I mean, he should probably know what's going on, right?"

"What's going on, Johnson? Nothing's going on, right?" Thorne replied.

"Not a thing," Gilday added.

"Nothing, we're not even gonna talk to the guy, Bill," Scroggins said.

"We just want to see that he's there," said Thorne.

"I don't know, he's gonna be mad, you know how he is."

"Come on, Bill," Scroggins leaned forward. "Why put the captain's cock in a lock over nothing? We're just going to check on the guy."

"I don't know, he could …" Johnson pulled the van into the parking lot of the hospital.

"Bill, shut up," Gilday said. "Just do as you're told."

"Time to get hands-on. Park in the back," Thorne said. "Everybody follow me and let me do the talking."

CHAPTER 17

Moments later, all five of them, Thorne, Kane, Gilday, Scroggins and Johnson, followed a visibly flustered doctor down the hall of the hospital.

"Like I told the officer on the phone," the doctor said, "this is a very secure building, there's no way in or out of this wing without any of the staff seeing you. We have regular bed-checks and …"

"I want to see for myself. I'm a federal officer so stop fucking with me, understand?" Thorne cut him off. "If I have to get a warrant, I'm going to put a boot to your ass and kick you into the middle of next week."

They stopped at the entrance to the Psych Ward, where a nurse sat in a window and eyed them curiously. The entrance door to the ward was large, heavy and locked electronically, Kane noted. The only way in was to be buzzed through by the nurse on duty.

"Doctor," Kane said, "just let us verify it with our own eyes and then we'll go, I promise. There's a lot at stake here, another young girl has been killed. We just want to see."

The doctor took a deep breath. "All right. But you must be quiet, these are all damaged people that need peace and quiet. Buzz them in, Beatrice."

The nurse pressed the buzzer to open the door and everyone entered the ward. The door shut and locked behind them. Kane lagged behind and noted that it was not physically possible for anyone to reach through the window of the Nurse's Station and hit the buzzer; it was too far out of reach. Kevin Durant wouldn't even be able to do it. She quickly caught up to the group.

"Mr. Robertson is in room twelve, it's around the corner down at the end."

"Do you have fire exits on this wing?" Thorne asked.

"Shh. Of course we do, but they're locked, they only open in the event the fire alarm goes off, or if someone buzzes from central. If the fire doors do open, an alarm goes off."

"Scroggins, Gilday, check them out. Kane, stay with me and keep Johnson out of trouble."

Scroggins tossed a radio to Kane and he and Gilday disappeared down the stair door.

Thorne, Kane and Johnson followed the doctor around a couple of turns in the hallway and finally stopped at room twelve. The doctor gestured to the window in the hospital room door. There was a figure sleeping in the bed.

"See?" the doctor whispered. "I told you he was here."

"His door locked?" Thorne asked.

"Of course not, why?"

Thorne opened the door to the hospital room. The doctor grabbed his arm.

"What are you doing? You can't disturb him!"

"Doc," Thorne said, "he's not breathing."

The doctor glanced at the sleeping figure, entered the room and carefully approached the bed.

"Ryan?" he whispered. "Ryan, wake up."

The doctor pulled back the sheets. Underneath the sheets were pillows and balled up clothes.

"So much for the bed-check," Kane said.

"Doc, you ought to be ashamed of yourself," Thorne said. "That trick is so old it should be on Viagra, that's how old that trick is."

The doctor, not amused, pushed past them at the doorway.

"Beatrice, call security!" The doctor rushed down the hallway.

"Now we have to find him," Kane said.

"No, we don't," Thorne corrected her.

"We don't? Why, you know where he is?"

"I don't know where he is, but I know where he's going to be soon. He's going to coming right back here to this room."

"Thorne, Kane," the radio on Kane's belt suddenly spoke. "You better come down here," It was Gilday.

Thorne took off at a good clip down the hall, Kane close behind. Johnson just stood there in awe of the empty bed in the hospital room.

"Johnson, let's go, young man, time's wasting!" Thorne barked from down the hall. Johnson jumped and scurried after them.

Some moments later, Thorne and Kane joined Gilday and Scroggins outside the back of the hospital, where they were standing next to a very open fire door. Johnson, huffing and puffing, soon followed.

"Ah, look at this, the locked fire door is somehow unlocked," said Thorne.

"Not just unlocked, but you can open and close it, no alarm, nothing," Scroggins demonstrated.

Kane examined the door. "How'd he do it?" she asked and found a gum wrapper lodged near the hinge. "What's this?"

"Foil from a gum wrapper, kept the magnetic charge constant," Gilday said. "But how'd he know how to do that?"

"Probably saw it in a movie," Thorne said.

"*Beverly Hills Cop II*. Good flick," said Scroggins.

"Damn good flick," Johnson agreed.

"So where he is now? What time is it?" Kane asked.

"Quarter to six," Gilday answered.

"Shit, we've been out at this all fucking night," Johnson grumbled.

"Sun will be up in about forty minutes," Scroggins said. "He has to show up soon. He's probably got a routine down, slip in right before shift change, something like that. He's gotta come back, unless he knows we're on to him."

"You know what I'd really like to know" Thorne asked.

"What?" said Kane.

"What I'd like to know is, how's he getting around? Doesn't drive, how did he get from here to Garrison?"

"There's somebody walking out of the woods," Johnson said, his voice a little shaky.

They all froze.

A dark figure stepped out of the woods surrounding the back parking lot about fifty yards away. The figure, that of a young man in snow gear, slid down the snow piled up high on the edge of the parking lot and made his way across the lot. Thorne slowly backed everyone away from the exit door and into the shadows.

"Keep still, let him get closer," Thorne whispered.

The man made it about halfway across the parking lot and suddenly stopped.

"Shit. He spotted us. He's gonna go OJ," Thorne whispered.

The man turned around and ran for the woods.

"He's going OJ!" Thorne started running but slipped on the ice and nearly fell.

Scroggins and Gilday pulled their weapons and ran like mad after the young man, Kane not far behind. Johnson stood dumb for a minute before starting after them. Thorne grabbed Johnson's arm before he got too far.

"Van, start the van!" Thorne yelled.

Johnson dug into his pocket for the keys, fumbled and dropped them. Thorne picked them up and jumped into the van, Johnson behind him. Robertson disappeared into the woods. Scroggins, Gilday and Kane floundered up the snow ditch piled on the edge of the parking lot. An engine roared.

Robertson revved his snowmobile and used the snow ditch to jump right over them, almost taking their heads off. He spun the snowmobile around in a circle and headed for the parking lot exit. Scroggins and Gilday fired their weapons at him and missed. Thorne started the van and gunned it before Johnson could shut the passenger door.

Thorne slid the van over to Gilday, Scroggins and Kane, the door open. They all piled in and Thorne gunned the engine again. The snowmobile zipped out of the parking lot exit. Thorne bounced the van off of a few parked cars on his way out of the lot in pursuit.

"Just anybody can drive one of those things, no license or nothing?" Thorne yelled as he cranked the van into a turn, just missing a ditch.

"Anybody, even kids!" Johnson yelled. "Watch the … watch the road, you can't go this fast!"

The van slipped and slid down a narrow county road after the fast-moving snowmobile, which skied through the snowy ditches next to the road with ease. Thorne cranked the wheel and barely made another turn, keeping parallel with Robertson.

"Where's he going, where's he going?" Thorne struggled to control the sliding van. Kane braced herself on the ceiling of the van.

"He's going for the river, he knows we can't follow him there!" yelled Scroggins.

"This little cocksucker is not getting away from me!" Thorne gritted his teeth.

"Watch out for the ..." Kane began.

The snowmobile vaulted the ditch and jumped across the road right in front of the van. Thorne swerved and just barely missed the snowmobile. The van slid into a one hundred-eighty-degree turn before flipping onto its side and sliding into the ditch. It kept sliding on its side until stopped with an ugly crunch by a tree.

The driver's side door opened and Thorne climbed out, weapon drawn. He jumped off of the van and ran for the road, but Robertson and his snowmobile were both long gone.

"FUCK!" Thorne screamed.

Scroggins climbed out of the driver's side door. He stooped to help Kane out. The back doors of the van opened, tumbling Gilday and Johnson out into the snow.

"Fuck shit piss cocksucker! Goddamn it!" Thorne continued his tirade.

"Everybody okay?" Scroggins asked. "Jeff, Bill? Bill, you're bleeding."

Johnson touched his forehead, finding blood. He got paler, if at all possible, and quickly sat down on a convenient bank of snow. Gilday took a look at the cut.

"It's okay, couple stitches probably," Gilday said.

The radio on Scroggins's belt crackled and he put it to his ear.

"Well," Kane brushed herself off, "at least we know for sure who he is, right?"

"Fucking pock-marked asshole!" Thorne kicked the van.

"Shit!" Scroggins got everyone's attention. "Hey, guys, he just snatched another kid, not five minutes ago. At a school bus stop, drove right up, knocked down the mom, grabbed the kid and drove off. They lost them in the woods along the river. Positive ID."

"He knows we're onto him so he's gonna have one last hurrah," Gilday said. "But where's he going?"

Something just over Gilday's shoulder grabbed Thorne's attention. Gilday turned to see what was. Off in the distance were Brainard's grain silos.

Gilday turned back to Thorne.

"Are you up for a little Dungeons and Dragons?" Thorne asked him with a grin.

Thorne didn't wait for an answer, just ran down the road toward the silos, Gilday close on his heels. Scroggins and Kane looked at each other and pulled their weapons. Johnson struggled to stand.

"What? What'd I miss?" Johnson asked, still wiping blood out of his eyes. "Where are we going?"

"Stay here," Scroggins pointed at him. "Call it in, he's going for the silos!"

CHAPTER 18

Thorne and Gilday arrived at the foot of the Brainard grain elevator, puffing from the run. It was still dark, though the morning sun was now beginning to make its presence felt. Brainard's grain silos were much larger than the silos in Garrison, at least five hundred feet in the air and additionally there were three of them.

Robertson's snowmobile sat right next to one of the steel trapdoors leading down into the ground. Gilday and Thorne threw open the gallery trapdoor just as Kane and Scroggins arrived. Thorne took out his flashlight.

A child's scream echoed from somewhere deep in the tunnels.

"Okay, kids, here's where it gets fun," Thorne grunted as he slid down the ladder to the darkness. Everyone followed. Kane could feel her pulse beat in her wrists and throat and struggled to control it.

Down in the tunnels, weapons ready, they all proceeded more cautiously. The concrete walls appeared to go on forever and this gallery was definitely bigger and more complex than the one they were in previously. The tunnel branched into two directions and they stopped at the intersection to get their bearings.

"Anyone by any chance know their way around down here?" Thorne whispered.

"No, man, all galleries are different," Scroggins replied. "They wind around and around and then back on themselves."

"Shit," Thorne sniffed. "All right, Staties go right, Federales go left. Stay salty and check your targets, if I get shot by one of you I will personally ruin your day."

The child's cry echoed through the tunnels again. Scroggins and Gilday ran the left tunnel and Thorne and Kane ran the one on the right.

Kane and Thorne came to a steel stairway and descended, only to arrive at another fork in their tunnel. In addition to the child's cries, they could hear Robertson cursing in the darkness. Kane sweated, despite the cold, and looked pale. Thorne motioned for her to take the branch on the left. Kane nodded and disappeared down her tunnel.

The cursing and crying got louder as Thorne followed his route. Thorne came to another steel stairway that opened out into a much larger space than the tunnel, the silo itself. A flashlight from below splashed across the concrete walls. Thorne carefully stepped onto the stairs, clicked off his flashlight and peered down below.

Robertson, back to Thorne, was on the floor below, cursing and tossing some equipment into a bag. A young girl sat against the wall and cried. Robertson was skinny, with lank greasy hair and a face cratered with acne.

Thorne checked out the environment. Multiple steel stairways on each wall led to the different levels of the gallery. Thorne noted the multiple exits on the floor below. Too many outs and Robertson probably knew them all.

Thorne would have to get close. His weapon poised, Thorne crept down the steel steps behind Robertson.

His shoes still covered with snow, Thorne slipped on the stairs just a few steps from the ground floor. He had to grab the railing to keep from falling and in doing so Thorne dropped his weapon. It clattered to the floor below.

Robertson spun and pulled out a nine-millimeter pistol. Thorne ducked back into the shadows. Robertson grabbed the little girl and held her in front of him as a shield.

"Who's there! Who's there, come out!"

Thorne spotted his weapon lying on the floor down below the stairs, in the shadows, well out of his reach. He cursed under his breath.

"Come out or else I'll fuckin' ..."

Thorne stepped quickly to the railing and waved.

"Hey, kid, how ya doing?" Thorne walked down the last few steps casually.

"Who are you!"

"Hey, easy, easy! Listen, if you and your sister want to camp out down here ..."

"Who are you?" Robertson cocked his pistol.

"Easy, easy!" Thorne reached into his jacket and flashed his identification at Robertson real quick. "Jacob Thorne, Nebraska Grain Association. Like I said, if you and your sister ..."

"Who?" Robertson asked. Thorne was now on the lower floor, facing Robertson. Thorne's weapon was not far away, still hidden in the shadows. He edged over to it.

"Jacob Thorne, Nebraska Grain Association. What's the gun for? Listen, I don't mean you and your sister any harm, honest."

"Nebraska Grain Association?" Robertson asked.

"Yeah, the Nebraska Grain Association. The NGA. You've

heard of it, right?" Thorne now stood right next to his weapon.

"Right," Robertson said after a moment and lowered his gun. Thorne casually started to bend down.

"Hold it," Robertson stopped him, bringing the nine back to bear on Thorne again. Thorne slowly straightened back up.

"What are you doing down here?" Robertson demanded.

Kane appeared in the exit behind Robertson, on his level. She aimed her weapon carefully at Robertson, mindful of the hostage.

Thorne saw that Kane had a clear shot, smiled and raised his hands.

"Checking the grain, there's been some reports …" Thorne said. "Listen, if you and your sister want to camp out down here, it's no skin off my ass, I'm just here for the grain. Could you lower that thing, guns make me nervous. What's the gun for?"

The end of Kane's pistol shook. She had trouble holding the target.

"It's a dangerous world," Robertson slid the little girl behind him and lowered his weapon. "A man needs some protection."

"Brother, I hear ya. But like I said, I'm just here to look at some grain."

A short but very pregnant pause followed this exchange. The end of Kane's pistol shook uncontrollably. The little girl cried silently. Robertson stared at Thorne with more suspicion.

Scroggins and Gilday suddenly appeared on the upper stairs, one level up, to Robertson's right.

"Robertson, drop the weapon now!" Scroggins ordered.

Robertson turned and fired his weapon up at Scroggins

and Gilday. Bullets ricocheted off the walls in their tunnel, wounding and stunning both men.

Robertson saw Kane behind him and fired at her. She ducked just in time and the bullets whined overhead. Kane fell on her rear and dropped her weapon. It bounced away, too far for her to reach.

Kane dead in his sights, Robertson chambered another round.

"Hey, Ryan, wait a second!" Thorne said.

Robertson whirled back around and pointed his weapon at Thorne's face. Robertson held the girl by her hair. Thorne stood in the exact same spot he was before.

"Easy, easy," Thorne said. "You know what, Ryan? I lied to you before, I'm sorry. I'm not with the Nebraska Grain Association. You want to know who I really am?"

"Who?" Robertson asked.

Thorne quickly raised his weapon and fired three times, hitting Robertson in the chest. Robertson flew backwards, hit the wall and fell to the floor. The little girl stood with her hands over her ears, crying.

"I am Shane," Thorne said.

Thorne walked over and calmly kicked Robertson's weapon away from his body.

"We're clear down here, clear!" he said.

Kane stood, went quickly to the little girl and picked her up. As she held the girl, Kane looked at Thorne for a moment before dropping her eyes. Gilday and Scroggins clambered down the stairs. Gilday's face bled, as did Scroggins's left arm. They both went to check Robertson's body.

Lights splashed over the walls of the space, coming from the level above. Voices and sirens could be heard.

"Cavalry's here finally," Thorne said, looking up. "Status?"

"We're bleeding but alive and mobile," Gilday replied.

"This piece of shit is still alive," Scroggins exclaimed over Robertson.

"Three slugs and he's still alive? Well, fine by me," Thorne said. "Now the parents of the kids he killed can be there when he gets the needle. Hey. You know what?"

"What?" Gilday asked.

"I'm hungry," Thorne said. "You guys up for some flapjacks?"

CHAPTER 19

Kane sat by herself at a table in the cafeteria of Brainard Memorial Hospital, an untouched tray of food in front of her. Gilday, bandages on his face, entered the cafeteria and walked over to Kane.

"Hey, Emma."

"Hey, Jeff, how are you?"

"Just scratched," he replied, "cement chips from the ricochet. Gerry got a chunk of it in his arm, but he's all right. They're gonna cut him loose soon."

"Good," Kane said, toying with her food.

Thorne entered the cafeteria carrying a tray loaded with food. He plopped it down across from Kane, sat and started to dig in.

"Hospital food, it sucks. It's so bad it's a wonder anyone ever gets well," Thorne said as he chewed.

"Hey, Thorne. Guess who I ran into upstairs, checking on Gerry?" Gilday said.

"Who?"

"Captain Forsythe."

"Yeah? Did he look constipated?"

"Now that you mention it, I think he did, yeah."

"Good."

Gilday watched Kane for a moment before nodding good-bye. "Okay then, I'll see you guys at HQ." Thorne and Kane nodded back to him and Gilday left.

They sat alone for a moment with the only sound of Thorne chewing as company. Thorne reached for the salt just as Forsythe walked by the doorway of the cafeteria, stopped and stared at them. They stared back.

"Fucking cowboys," Forsythe shook his head and continued on his way.

"He does look constipated," Thorne remarked. He ate in silence for a while.

"Aren't you going to say something?" Kane asked finally.

"About what?"

"About me, losing it. Not taking the shot. We're always supposed to take the shot. I had the shot. I got the shakes and didn't take the shot."

"Yeah, I noticed that."

"Aren't you going to say something?"

"Should I say something?"

"You usually do. Isn't this where you say something nasty about me being weak and girly and that they shouldn't send a woman to do a man's job, some kind of shit like that?"

"Hey, if you say it then I don't need to. We nailed Funny-Pants, that's the only thing I care about."

"Seriously? You're not going to nail me with some smart-ass sexist remark?"

"Not right now. I'm on a shoot-a-serial-killer high," Thorne said. "But don't worry, I'll get around to it later. Right now I just want to eat and enjoy my buzz."

"Well," Kane said after a moment, "there is one other thing. You saved my life. Thank you."

Thorne looked at Kane, chewing. He swallowed and

smiled at her. "That must have cost you, having to say that to me."

"It does, you're right. I wasn't looking forward to it."

"Well, don't let it go to your head. There wasn't anything personal about it, I just didn't want to have to deal with all the paperwork involved if you got yourself killed."

"I should've known."

They sat in silence. Kane pushed the food on her plate around with a fork.

"You were really on fire about Robertson. If we hadn't have beaten him back here to the hospital, he'd be sitting behind a lawyer and a decent alibi."

"He's small potatoes," Thorne grunted.

"Still, it was good to see you get going. I was beginning to wonder if all the talk about you was just that, talk."

"You know what I'm wondering about?" Thorne asked.

"What??

"You."

"Me?"

"You. Gonzo cop, attitude and balls to spare. Says so in your file."

"You read my file?"

"I read your file. Expert marksman, black belt, the works. Smarter than most, too, at least according to all the tests they give you rookies these days. It also says that while you were working undercover in DC, you shot and killed three men."

"True. So?" Kane shifted a bit.

"So why now the shakes? Hotdog like you? Never saw that coming."

"I thought that you knew everything."

"I didn't say I knew everything. I said that I'm always right. There's a difference."

"What's the difference?"

"Knowing everything is knowing everything," Thorne

said. "Being always right is knowing what you KNOW, knowing what you DON'T know, knowing what you NEED to know and then defining the relationship between all three of them. That's what always being right is."

Kane pondered that. "I see. And you think that there might be something that you need to know about me?"

"Hey, if they're going to give you a weapon and tell me that I've got to run around in the dark with you, then yeah, there might be a few things that I'd like to know about."

"Such as?"

"I think that there was a lot more to the DC story than what was in the file. I'd like to know what that more is."

"Would you?"

"I would."

"That works both ways. I'd like to know why you were retired off of the Mercy Killings."

Thorne finished his meal and slid the tray away.

"Show you mine and you'll show me yours, is that what you're getting at?" he asked.

"If you'll remove any and all sexual connotations from that observation, then yes, that's exactly what I'm getting at."

Thorne sniffed and shrugged. "All right, why not?"

"You first."

"Why do I have to go first?"

"Age before beauty."

Thorne snorted. "First, you tell me what you know about the Mercy Killings so far," he said.

"Mercy killings," Kane sat up a little straighter. "Biggest case in the Bureau, biggest case in the country and maybe the biggest case in the history of murder. There are more people working on it than anything else. Single killer, been operating five years or so. He has over a hundred kills that we know of, from all over the United States.

"The size of his Kill Zone is one thing that makes him

unusual. He has confirmed kills in over twenty different states. Once in awhile the victims are forced to write MERCY on whatever's near, hence the name the Mercy Killer, but he doesn't do that every time. He takes the tongues of his victims. He last struck in Georgia, about two weeks ago, a clerk at a copy store. That's what I know. Not much gossip gets out from the brain trust running the case. They're keeping it tight even among law enforcement. Case is a media carnival. There's already been two cable movies made about him, a mini-series, a bunch of books and who knows what else. The Mercy Killer is bigger than Ted Bundy, Jack the Ripper and the DC snipers all rolled into one. That's what I know."

"He is the biggest, bar none," Thorne cracked his knuckles with relish. "The Shaquille O'Neal of serial killers.

"Around the campfire they call him Kevorkian, or at least we did in the beginning," Thorne continued. "We eventually got official memos not to refer to the killer as Kevorkian ever, not even informally in communication with each other, and some guys got letters of censure for doing so, yours truly being one of them. Fuck it, Kevorkian is a much better tag for him than the Mercy Killer, that's what I always thought.

"When it comes to the killing, he varies his MO. Sometimes he stabs, sometimes he strangles, he's done just about everything you can imagine and then some when it comes to murder. Taking the tongue is his signature. That never changes. We've never recovered any of the tongues, ever. The other thing that makes him unusual is his range of victims.

"His taste in vics is wide and varied, many different professions, though he does seem to favor salesmen and postal workers more than most, in addition to a few local cops. But his choice of victims transcends race, sex, age, just about everything, which I don't have to tell you is rare, very rare.

"His timeline for killing has no real rhythm to it; he'll take out five in one week and then go a month without doing anything. We don't know how he selects his victims and more importantly, we can't figure out why or what he's trying to accomplish by killing them and taking their tongues. Nobody can quite figure out the WHAT or the WHY of this case, hell, we haven't even had a lot of success with WHERE. He crisscrosses the country. We know he likes to kill face to face and we know he follows his press coverage, even though there is almost too much of it to keep track of.

"Here's an interesting story about Kevorkian that not many folks know about. Second year in, one of the murders we were investigating in New Jersey turned out to be the work of a copycat. I caught it right away, the guy was even more inept than Robertson was. We linked the copycat to the vic but before we could even get warrants, Kevorkian got him."

"Kevorkian killed the copycat?" Kane asked.

"Within a day, before we could even move on him, before we could even bring him in for questioning, his tongue was gone and he was dead. I guess Kevorkian was displeased that somebody else was pissing in his yard. Too bad this Iceman character wasn't as motivated when it came to FunnyPants, it would have saved us a lot of running around in the snow."

"Do you think that it matters to the Iceman, his copycat?"

"Oh yeah, it matters. If the Iceman could have figured out who FunnyPants was, then he would have done something about it. Granted, it didn't take a genius to figure out who Kevorkian's copycat killer was, any local homicide investigator would have eventually busted him. But Kevorkian was on him quick, like stink on shit, he was that fast.

"It was the first real glimpse we've had into Kevorkian's character. His ego. His ego is large. This guy is off the charts, we don't have anyone like him on the books and that's why it's been so fucking hard to catch him. Rarely leaves any consistent forensic evidence, very rarely. Makes the Iceman look positively sloppy. What's the first rule of forensic science?"

"Every contact leaves a trace," Kane answered.

"Every contact leaves a trace, that's it. Well, Kevorkian seems to be onto that one. Trace is varied and oftentimes deliberately misleading. I was lead profiler on the case, three years, when I got retired."

"What happened, why were you retired?" Kane asked.

"The ASAC on the case, the guy I was reporting to, he got himself perished."

"Killed?"

"Dead and tongueless."

"Kevorkian killed the ASAC running your case?"

"Not just him, either. He also tagged the ASAC's boss, the Special Agent in Charge of the whole shebang, one day later. Kevorkian killed two federal agents, not just investigators, but the ones running the show, just like that, one-two-bing-bing."

"I don't fucking believe it," Kane said. "Wait a minute, I remember this when it happened, but the news said they were killed in a car accident."

"The news also said that the real reason we invaded Iraq was to free the Iraqi people."

"How can you ... do you know for certain that it was him?"

"Absolutely certain, I vetted both crime scenes. I was there. He killed them and they covered it up."

"I don't fucking ... how could they do that?"

"Come on, Kane, you work for the government now, wake up. They can do whatever ever they want to do and spin it however they want to spin it. We can put whatever story we want in the news, regardless of how true it is, we can arrest and detain anyone we want for as long as we wish without giving them access to counsel, hell, we can step outside right now, shoot the first person we see and call them a threat to Homeland Security and make it stick. This is the federal government, wake up and smell the coffee.

"The director decided that he did not want word to get out that some serial killer killed the federal officers chasing him; he felt that it might reflect badly upon the Bureau. So he squashed it, sent out a press release saying the two men were killed in an unfortunate car accident and that was that. The families went along with it and the men were buried with honors.

"Kevorkian has killed a number of local cops in different states at differing levels of authority and some with none at all. But this was the first time he went federal and it scared everybody. Shit hit the fan, heads rolled and mine was one of them."

"They retired you because your boss got murdered? But you'd think that now they'd need everyone they could get," Kane said.

"Let's just say that I am less than popular with the ambitious blue flaming circles within the Bureau. When I was brought onboard the investigation, there was a lot of political bullshit flying around, which I never had time for or gave a fuck about. I guess you could say that I stepped on a few toes."

"You? I can't imagine that," Kane said.

"Hard to believe, I know, but it's true. I ruffled a few feathers. Particularly with the next man they put in charge of the case, Richard MacVey. We had some history. I made him look like an ass some years ago, more than once, and he paid me off for it.

"In the past, the director always put up with my shit

because I produced. I was the best. I got results. I caught the shitbird. Since I hadn't produced or caught anybody while on the Kevorkian case, then they had no reason to put up with my shit. They cut me loose, almost a year ago, and it pleased MacVey to no end."

"Jesus Christ."

"Well, he thought he was. Now we'll never know; he also got himself killed in a 'car accident' and de-tongued just a few days ago."

"What?"

"Yeah, Kevorkian is making life difficult for those trying to catch him, the prick. Let me tell you something, I was just starting to get the scent, too. I didn't have anything solid but I was just getting that whiff when I got put out to pasture."

"You thought you were close?"

"I thought I was close to being close."

"Were you ever afraid that he might come after you?" Kane asked.

"Let him. I hope he does. Fucker got me fired."

"So if you catch the Iceman, you get another shot at Kevorkian, the guy that cost you your job."

"Correct-a-mundo," Thorne said. "Now then. Quid pro quo, Clarice. I showed you mine."

Kane took a deep breath, collecting herself.

"You read the file, so you know the basics. Eighteen months ago, somebody was raping, torturing and killing prostitutes. I was working decoy. We had a suspect, we knew his van from some sketchy witnesses' statements and we knew his favorite hunting spots. We had blue carpet fiber from one of the victims, but it wasn't even enough for a warrant. My job was to get a look in the van. I wasn't to go inside the van under any circumstances, just get a look. If I saw blue carpeting, then we'd go for the warrant.

"I was in one of his favorite spots and we figured it would be hard for him to pass me up. We spot the van coming and sure enough, he pulls over next to me. Only there were two men in the van instead of one. I got a good look at them. The driver was scraggly-haired and dirty, missing a tooth. The other guy was short, really short, with a lot of tattoos. He was sitting in the passenger seat. The little guy asked me if I wanted to party.

"I wasn't even armed. I was wired but because of the skimpy hooker get-up there was literally no place for me to stash a piece. That's why I wasn't supposed to get into the van. My backup was only a block away. We figured I would be all right. Of course, no one figured that there would be two guys instead of one.

"And nobody figured that it would be more than two guys. The side door of the van opened and this huge fat guy with a shaved head jumped out. Three guys doing this shit. Baldy told me to get in, they would pay top dollar so get my ass in the van.

"The floor of the van was covered in blue carpeting. Once Baldy opened the door and I saw the carpeting, I knew I had what I needed and I just had to get out of there. I told them I'd take a rain check and started to walk away. The little guy in the passenger seat pulled out a gun and pointed it at me. Baldy called me a whore.

"They grabbed me, tossed me in the van and took off right then and there, and there was nothing my backup could do about it except try and catch up. The freeway was less than a quarter mile away and they got on it. Once we were on the freeway, I knew I was fucked.

"They handcuffed me to separate bars that were conveniently welded on the wall of the van. They were thorough; they used two sets of handcuffs to secure me. They fucking had me good. I wasn't the only one they had in the van, either.

"They had another girl, real young, maybe fourteen or fifteen years old, tops. Probably a runaway that started to turn tricks to survive, looked innocent enough that she hadn't been doing it very long. She was handcuffed to the other side of the van. They'd ripped her clothes off and from the looks of things, they'd already raped her more than once. She was bleeding. She was crying. They brought out their party kit and showed it to us.

"They told us, in great detail, just exactly what they were going to do. The little guy with the gun had a video camera, recording the whole thing. The big guy got out the pliers and started working on the girl. She screamed. Terrible screams. I told them I was a cop. Didn't matter to them. The little guy pistol-whipped me.

"They ripped the wire off. Slapped me around some more. They wanted me to watch, so that I would know what was in store for me next. They went back to work on the girl, this time with knives. They killed her very slowly, giggling the whole time while she screamed. After she was dead, they turned their attention to me.

"They ripped my clothes off. I got hysterical," Kane took another deep, deep breath.

"I got more than hysterical. I lost my shit. I begged them. They laughed. I remember how they laughed. I'll always remember how they laughed."

"How'd you get out of it?" Thorne asked, his eyes bright. Kane was far away as she relived her story.

"Somehow I pulled my right hand out through the cuff. Dislocated my thumb. My left hand was still handcuffed to the side of the van. I got my right free and then I started fighting for my life. I punched Baldy in the throat.

"The little guy pointed the gun at me and I grabbed hold of it. I trapped his gun hand and flipped him down on the floor, wrapping my legs around his neck, choking the shit out of him.

"I got the gun away from the little guy and I just started shooting. Baldy was just getting his breath back. He came at me. I shot Baldy, I shot him in the crotch.

"Then I shot the driver, even though we were going down the highway at seventy miles an hour, I shot him right in the back of the head. Blood went all over the windshield and the van started swerving back and forth.

"Then I shot the little guy. I had him in a judo choke and immobilized, but I shot him anyway. I remember him saying 'please don't' before I fired. That's one of the many things probably not in the report. I shot him in the face. I shot him more than once. I got drenched in the spray.

"As luck would have it, we were going over a bridge on the freeway when I shot the driver. The van went off the bridge and into the river. The van hit the river and water starts to pour into the interior of the van. I'm still handcuffed by my left hand to the wall of the van. I dig through the pockets of the little guy, he's the only one I can reach, and I'm praying that he's got the keys to the cuffs. Water was coming in fast, it was up past my chest, and I thought for sure I was going die in that van. I found the keys, unlocked the cuffs and made for the door. I kicked the backdoors open. Then I saw him. The big guy, Baldy, he was still alive. He grabbed me as I tried to swim out. This part is definitely not in the report.

"For some reason, I was still holding the set of the hand-cuffs. I locked one side of the cuffs around his wrist. I locked the other side of the cuffs to the van. I cuffed him to the van and then I swam out the back door. I left him there, alive and bellowing at me.

"I could have brought him out, but I didn't. I let him go down. I didn't shoot him. I left him there. I let him drown. I let him drown slow. I swam to the bank of the river, naked, stood there and watched him go down. My backup arrived two minutes later.

"The mayor's office spun it so that I was a hero, but I wasn't. I could have forced them to stop the van once I got the gun. I didn't."

"You killed them instead," Thorne said.

"I did. I didn't have to."

"But you did."

"I did. I executed them. No arrest, no trial. Just started shooting. I executed them. I didn't have to but I did."

"And it bothers you?" Thorne asked.

"Hell yes, it bothers me."

"Why does it bother you?"

"Because."

"Because why? Afraid you lost your edge?"

"It bothered me because of how it made me feel. When I shot them. I didn't want to ever feel that way again," Kane said. "I've had the shakes ever since then, even on the firing range."

Thorne leaned back, looking at Kane for a long moment.

"That's why you became a profiler, that's why you joined ISU. Profilers almost never fire their weapons."

"And then they stick me with a cowboy like you," Kane said, her face impassive.

"Yeah, how about that?"

"How about that?"

"Not that I disagree with your assessment of my character, but today was the first time I've ever fired my weapon in the line of duty," Thorne said.

"This was the first time you shot a suspect?"

"Yep."

"Does it bother you?"

"The only thing that bothers me is that he lived through it, the lucky bastard."

"You've never killed anyone?"

"I've killed. I've caught a lot of dirty fuckers, sat their ass on death row and made sure I was there when they got the needle. I sat there, watched them die in their own piss and shit without a single problem."

"Felt just fine about it, did you?"

"I felt more than fine. But you, we're talking about you and how you felt when you shot Baldy and his buddies."

"Is that what we were talking about?"

"This feeling you felt when you killed them, the one you never wanted to feel again. Describe it for me."

"Did I tell you that I was a chess champion in high school?"

"Describe this feeling you felt."

"I've said enough, Thorne," Kane said. "I've held up my end of the deal. Let's get back to HQ and get moving on Iceman. He's still out there and he has Wendy Frederickson. She might still be alive while you and I sit here and shoot the shit with each other."

Thorne stared at her for a moment. He stood and stretched, popping joints in his neck and shoulders.

"Wendy Frederickson is dead."

"She's dead?"

"She was dead within twenty-four hours of her abduction."

"How do you know that?" Kane asked.

"How do I know anything??

"You're sure Wendy Frederickson is dead?"

"That's what I said, isn't it?"

"I know, but how …"

"I wouldn't have said it if I wasn't sure."

"What are we going to do next?"

"I'm going to take a piss and after I do that, we're heading back to the office and you're going to type up the after-action report on Robertson," Thorne replied.

"What are we going to do about the Iceman?" Kane asked. "You haven't said much of anything about him, when are you going to profile him?"

"When I'm ready. Timing is everything, Kane."

"What if he snatches another girl?"

"He has to drop Frederickson before he grabs someone else. I'm tired of talking so leave me alone."

"He doesn't always drop them, sometimes he …"

"He'll drop this one, now will you shut up? I have to piss like a foaming racehorse and you're making me crazy."

Thorne walked away from Kane. He stopped a few steps away and turned back.

"Pulled your hand right through a handcuff, did you?"

"Yes."

"That explains the scars," Thorne said.

"Yeah," Kane said, looking at her right hand, "I still have the scars."

CHAPTER 20

"I should get hazard pay, Pete," Thorne said into the telephone. "You didn't tell me this was a two-fer. Do I get extra credit for it? I'd fucking better. Yeah. Girl Friday will be emailing you the report as soon as she's done. What?

"How's the local PD treating us? They're a bunch of backward-ass country fucks, how do you think they're treating us? I've seen better heads on a glass of beer."

Various uniformed personnel from nearby desks stared in Thorne's direction sourly after this last remark, but decided to let it pass. Kane looked up from her desk, where she was typing a report on a computer.

"I can handle 'em, don't worry about it. Well, there isn't much to do at the moment, the Task Force commander here has some black guy he likes that he wants to charge and he's going to shit a brick when DNA comes back negative. Hell yeah, I'm sure, why does everyone keep asking me that, would I say so if I weren't?

"Yeah. Well, I'm thinking about that right now as we speak. I'll crack it, no worries, and then I want yours. What's the latest? What? No shit? I hope you're sleeping with your Glock under your pillow, Pete. Okay. All right. Talk to you," Thorne hung up the phone and stared at his chessboard. He felt Kane's gaze on the back of his neck.

"Kevorkian hit in New York City while you were there with Pete to pick me up. They just found the body this morning," Thorne said without looking at her.

"What? Who?"

"Cab driver, time of death was sometime on the day we left, according to the coroner. They just found him and his cab. Neck broken. No tongue. Pete knows for sure he's being shadowed by the guy now."

Thorne made a move on the chessboard and turned the board around to play from the other side. Gilday and Scroggins, arm in a sling, walked over to Kane and Thorne.

"I thought you two were taking the day off?" Kane asked.

"No way, not while the Iceman's out and about," Gilday replied. "We're pumped now. We want his ass next."

"Hey, Thorne," Scroggins said. "You should have seen Forsythe's face when he found out you cracked up the van. Turned purple and blue."

"Yeah? Where is that big turd, anyway? He's got some serious crow coming his way, big time."

"He's sweating Robertson in the box. I don't think they told you, Robertson was wearing a vest," Gilday said.

"A bulletproof vest? Somebody remind me to go for the head shot next time."

"He had all sorts of fun toys down in his little playpen," Gilday said.

"Anything good?" Kane asked.

"We got a lot of physical evidence, some knives which help, and a shotgun in addition to his pistol. A confession would be good, though, that's why Forsythe's sweating him."

"And?" Thorne looked up.

"He's talking but not admitting anything. Hasn't asked for a lawyer, claims he's innocent and that us cops are trying to frame him," Gilday replied.

"He really is going OJ on us," Thorne said. "They going to crack him?"

"I don't know," Scroggins admitted. "Hard to tell, he's a nut. Once he lawyers up, he'll probably go insanity and that'll be that."

"No fucking way," Thorne stood. "Get me a shot at him."

"Right, the captain would love that. Forget it."

"I can crack that nut, get me in there."

"You shot the guy," Gilday said. "How are you going to crack him?"

"Easy as pie, trust me. I can do it. I want this cupcake going all the way to the chair for all five murders; he's not doing easy mental time on my shift. Call your buddy the gov, throw some weight around. Get me in that room and I'll get it, I'm telling you."

Gilday looked at Scroggins and shrugged. "Well, Captain's already unhappy with us, why not go all the way and totally piss him off?"

"What the hell, it's only a career."

"I'll get on the horn now," Gilday picked up the phone.

"Hey, Gerry, I have a question," Kane asked. "How does a mental patient who can't even get a driver's license somehow obtain a bulletproof vest, a shotgun and a nine-millimeter Glock?"

"Welcome to Nebraska," Scroggins replied.

"It's worse in Texas," Gilday said.

CHAPTER 21

An hour later, Thorne and Kane entered the anteroom to interrogation, where Gilday and Scroggins watched Forsythe and Hairston question Robertson through a one-way mirrored window. A video camera was placed right up against the mirror-window of the anteroom to record everything inside interrogation.

Robertson, handcuffed to a chair inside the stark room and very angry, screamed at Forsythe. Kane wondered about a briefcase Thorne held in one hand. She'd asked him about it but he avoided answering.

"So your pal the governor came through," Thorne said.

"He did," Gilday said. "But you should have heard the screaming from this end."

"How they doing?" Thorne gestured to Forysthe.

"Not good."

"He still says he's innocent and being framed," Gilday replied. "Blames the government for everything."

"Me too," Thorne said.

"Hey, Emma," Scroggins smiled.

"Hey, Emma," Gilday followed suit.

"Jeff, Gerry. How's the arm doing?"

"Still attached," Scroggins wriggled his fingers at her.

"Everybody back at HQ is avoiding us like we have anthrax. And they weren't all that friendly to begin with. What's going on?" Kane asked.

"Welcome to the Captain's Permanent Shit List," Gilday replied. "He's spread the word on you two, he's very displeased with the latest turn of events."

"Displeased? He wouldn't even have this guy if we weren't here!"

"And that's why he's pissed off," Gilday replied. "His people are supposed to make the collars, not you."

"He's not too happy with the two of us, either," Scroggins said. "If we didn't have friends in high places, we'd be completely out of the loop."

"What kind of bullshit is this? We're only here to help, how are we supposed to help if nobody gives us any information?" Kane demanded.

"Typical jurisdictional dispute. Forsythe wants the headlines. State case until the Iceman crosses state lines," Gilday said.

"Notice how he's been careful not to do that," Thorne said without turning.

"I mean, officially he welcomes federal support, he has to. But unofficially the policy is 'fuck you' without any ifs, ands or buts. We get shit like this on a local level all the time," Scroggins said. "Forsythe hands it over to you feds, it looks like he can't handle the case. He lets you crack it, same difference. Notice in the papers that you're always referred to as advisors."

"Now we can't even do that," Kane said, looking at Thorne's back. "Anything on Wendy Frederickson turn up yet?"

"Nothing," Scroggins replied. "We've got search teams

scouring the state, using bloodhounds and satellites, there are posters everywhere. They've turned up exactly zip."

"It's like she disappeared into thin air," Gilday said.

"She's close by. Within fifty miles," Thorne said.

"How do you know?" Kane asked.

"She's close by because the Iceman is close by. He's in the area. Wait, what's this guy doing now?"

Thorne pointed at Robertson through the window. Robertson spat violently at Forsythe and banged his head against the table repeatedly.

"He does that when he's angry. He can do it for hours," Scroggins said.

"Captain's trying to make it difficult for you," Gilday said. "How do you know that the Iceman's in the area?"

"I looked at the map."

Forsythe and Hairston exited interrogation and entered the anteroom.

"He's all yours, Agent Thorne," Hairston said.

"And I want to go on record that I'm against you meddling in this. We have the situation in hand," Forsythe fumed.

"You wouldn't have anything but your dick in your hand if it wasn't for his meddling," Kane said.

"Don't get smart, Missy, tits and ass only take you so far," Forsythe turned to Thorne. "He hasn't asked for a lawyer yet. We don't want him to ask for a lawyer. You fuck this up and I will make it my mission to ruin your life in whatever way that I can."

Thorne looked at Forsythe for a long moment.

"One of these days you and I are going to have a serious disagreement," Thorne said calmly.

Thorne picked up his briefcase and entered the interrogation room.

CHAPTER 22

Robertson stopped banging his head against the table when Thorne entered interrogation and sat down across the table from him. Thorne took out some gum and popped a stick into his mouth.

"Hey, Ryan, how are ya?"

"I didn't do anything!" Robertson yelled.

"I know."

"I didn't do anything!"

"I know. Gum?" Thorne offered the pack to Robertson.

"You shot me!"

"I know, I'm sorry. I thought you were someone else."

"You did?"

"I did, I'm sorry. Case of mistaken identity, I thought you were somebody else."

"Who?"

"I thought you were Mr. FunnyPants. Gum?" Thorne offered the pack again.

"Okay," Robertson said after a moment. Thorne took out a piece, unwrapped it and put it into Robertson's mouth for him.

"If I had known who you really were, I never would have shot you. You're okay, right? They told me you were wearing a vest, so no permanent damage, right?"

"My chest hurts, it's black and blue all over," Robertson pouted.

"I'm really sorry about that, I shouldn't have shot you, my mistake. You want to see a lawyer?" Thorne asked.

"A lawyer?"

"A lawyer, I can get you a lawyer if you want one, you want a court-appointed lawyer?" Thorne could almost hear Forsythe have a heart attack on the other side of the glass. Robertson thought about it for a minute.

"I don't trust lawyers," he said finally.

"You know what? Me neither," Thorne said.

"'Sides, I didn't do anything that I need a lawyer for, anyhow," Robertson said.

"Hey, if you say so, who am I to argue?"

"If I'm not the guy you're looking for, what's his name?"

"Mr. FunnyPants."

"If I'm not him, then what am I doing here?" Robertson asked.

"Well, I was hoping that you could help me with something. See, Ryan, somebody's been doing some killing."

"So?"

"You know what?" Thorne said. "I feel the same exact way you do, most of the time. I mean, let's face it, there are some very disagreeable people out there, right?"

"Right."

"There are some real miserable fucks out in the world that deserve to die, that's what I think. Nasty assholes that should be killed. Fuck 'em, right?"

"Yeah, fuck 'em," Robertson liked the turn this conversation has taken.

"You met the captain, right?" Thorne asked, putting a stick of gum into his own mouth.

"Who?"

"Big fat guy, shouts a lot. He was just in here."

"Oh yeah. I don't like him."

Thorne opened his briefcase and took pictures out of it, framed school pictures of the little girls Robertson had killed. Thorne propped them up on the table, just out of Robertson's reach. Robertson appeared somewhat uncomfortable.

"Me neither. He's a case in point," Thorne said. "A real gaping asshole, the captain. But the deal is, nobody's killing big mean bastards like him. At least not yet. But somebody HAS been killing these little girls."

"It's that guy, the guy in the papers."

"What guy?"

"The guy, the guy in the papers, they call him the Iceman. He's killing little girls," Robertson was definitely uncomfortable now.

"You're right, he is," Thorne said. "But not these girls. These girls, right here, were killed by somebody else. And I need to find whoever it is."

"Why? Can you put those away?"

"I was hoping you could look at these pictures and help me find this guy, Ryan."

"Why, what do you care? You said yourself, some people deserve to die."

"Yeah, some do. But not these girls. These are kids."

"So?" Robertson sneered.

"So it's innocent blood," Thorne said. "Innocent blood is being spilled and we have to act when that happens."

"Can you put those pictures away?"

"I need you to look at them for me."

"I don't want to look at them."

"Somebody's got innocent blood on his hands and we have to find him."

"What makes you so sure they're innocent?"

"They're just little kids, too young to be mean, miserable and nasty. Innocent."

"Shit," Robertson spit out his gum. "You don't know anything, do you?"

"What don't I know?"

"Put those away."

"What don't I know? It's innocent blood, Ryan."

"STOP FUCKING LOOKING AT ME!" Robertson lunged for the pictures but was halted by the bolted chair he was handcuffed to. He glared at Thorne.

"Innocent blood, my ass! Little kids are meaner and more miserable than anybody. ANYBODY! ESPECIALLY LITTLE FUCKING GIRLS! Don't you remember being a kid? Don't you remember how fucking cruel kids are? The things they'd say and do?"

"How they stared at you?" Thorne asked.

"Looking and laughing and pointing! Making fun. Little girls have no innocent blood in them. Especially the popular pretty ones. They're the worst!" Robertson rattled his chair, furious. "Put those away. PUT 'EM AWAY!"

"That's why you killed these girls? They wouldn't stop looking?" Thorne asked.

"I killed them because they deserved it. They deserved to be sliced up. They deserved what they got."

"You're not crazy, you knew exactly what you were doing, didn't you?"

"I did, I killed every one of these girls here and I'd do it again. I will. Just watch, I'll get 'em. I'll get 'em all back. Fuck 'em!" Robertson yelled, spittle spraying.

"I see."

"Now put those fucking things away!" Robertson demanded.

"I don't think so, Ryan," Thorne stood. "I think I'll let them watch you for a little while."

"NO!" Robertson screamed and rattled against his chair and handcuffs. Thorne winked and walked away.

Robertson continued to scream after Thorne exited and shut the door to the interrogation room carefully and quietly.

"Turn the camera off," Thorne said to Hairston. "Let him get stared at for awhile."

Everyone in the room was quiet as they watched Robertson rage on the other side of the glass.

"I'm hungry again, I'm going for some pizza," Thorne grabbed his coat. "Don't bother me unless it's real fucking important."

CHAPTER 23

Barb Mullens lifted her daughter Darcy up and set her on the kitchen counter to put the young girl's snow boots on. Darcy was seven and so cute that sometimes Barb was amazed, absolutely amazed, that this little girl had emerged from her.

Not that Barb had been a bad-looking kid herself, but nothing like Darcy. Lord knows Darcy didn't get her looks from her father. Chad looked good now but when he was young he was homely as all get out. If somebody had told Barb back in fourth grade that she would someday grow up and marry Chad Mullens, she would have been horrified. Chad really grew into his looks.

But Darcy, with her corn-silk blonde hair and bright blue eyes, she was a stunner from day one. And so good, a good kid too. Sometimes kids weren't good, no matter what the parents did, sometimes kids were just rotten. Not Darcy, she was sweet beyond compare. Barb tightened Darcy's left boot.

"All ready to go?" Barb asked.

"Ready to go!" Darcy said happily, further breaking Barb's heart. How many kids were happy to go to school?

"Remember the rules," Barb said, starting a now familiar routine. "After school's out, you wait INSIDE with Mrs. Goodwin until?"

"Until you pick me up!"

"Until you SEE me and I pick you up. Me or Dad, nobody else. What's next?"

"Don't ever talk to strangers!"

"And if anyone, ANYBODY, ever touches you in your private place, what do you do?"

"Tell you."

"Who else?"

"Tell Daddy."

"Who else?"

"Mrs. Goodwin, my teacher."

"Who else?" Barb looked at Darcy, who had to think about it for a minute. "There's one more person you can tell if someone does a bad thing. Who do you tell when somebody does something bad?"

Darcy got it. "A policeman!"

"Right! You can tell a policeman. Or a policewoman."

"Policewoman," Darcy repeated solemnly.

"That's my good girl," Barb kissed Darcy on her nose and lifted her down off the counter. "Let's get you to school."

CHAPTER 24

Thorne walked into headquarters, whistling as he shrugged his coat off and tossed it onto a chair next to his desk. Kane looked up bleary-eyed from her desk. She'd been there the whole night, studying the file and pictures, finally catching a few hours of shut-eye at the desk with her head in her arms right before dawn.

"Where were you all night?" Kane asked.

"In my room at the resplendent Budget Inn. Ordered a large meat-lovers pizza, crashed and watched some cable. They got all these forensic criminal dramas on television now, I like to watch them and giggle my ass off." Thorne sat in front of his chessboard and studied it. He clicked on his CD player and the excellent Etta James began to do her thing.

"So what, you basically took the night off?"

"You could say that."

"How could you do that? We still have another psycho out there holding a young girl, and you decide to pig out in front of the TV?"

"Yep."

"I can't believe you, you bust a nut going after Robertson,

running like mad in the snow, but when it comes to the Iceman and the Frederickson girl you inexplicably decide you need a break?"

"You haven't been listening, I thought you wanted to learn from me. I'm not going to repeat myself again. One, timing is everything. Two, the girl is already dead and there won't be much to do until he drops her, which he will do soon," Thorne said, concentrating on his chessboard.

"Besides, what did you accomplish staying up most of the night here, other than reviewing material you've already gone over again and again? You're like those pretty faces on those goofy fucking TV shows, making noise for no reason."

"Maybe I should take a break like you, catch a movie or something, next time we're in a car chase."

"As long as you're not driving, I don't care."

"I don't get you," Kane said.

"And who says you will?" Thorne replied, turning to face her. "I told you, it's all in the timing."

"Yeah, I heard you, but what the fuck does that mean?"

"Listen to this music, how do you think it fits together?" Thorne held out his hand toward the song Etta James was most definitely feeling on his CD player. "The music in a song isn't just simply the musical notes. It's the space in between them. A song without strategically placed rests, or any rests at all, isn't a song or music. Without the rests, without the timing, it's nothing. It's just noise. It's just TV."

Thorne turned his attention back to the chessboard. He made another move and turned the board around, viewing the situation from the other side. Kane watched him for a moment.

"Why do you do that?" Kane asked finally.

"Do what?"

"Play chess against yourself, you know that you're guaranteed to lose that way, don't you?"

"Also guaranteed to win."

"So what's the point?"

"You're just making noise now, Kane, you're bothering me. Why don't you go play with your friends, Bo and Luke Duke? Speak of the devil, here's the handsome bastards themselves."

Gilday and Scroggins, his arm no longer in a sling, entered headquarters and walked over to them.

"You might want to see this," Gilday turned on a nearby television. Forsythe's large frame appeared, Hairston close by his side, on the screen at a press conference.

"In addition to evidence linking him to five of the murders, we have been able to extract a confession from Ryan Robertson, admitting to the crimes," Forsythe took a dramatic pause. "We have determined that he is not responsible for any of the other disappearances or murders; in other words, he is NOT the criminal you all have labeled the Iceman."

"We? What's this WE shit?" Thorne grumbled.

"We do have a suspect in custody that we strongly believe is connected to the Iceman killings. We are waiting for the DNA results to come back from the lab before going before a grand jury. The search for Wendy Frederickson will continue until she is recovered. My task force and I will not rest until the man responsible for the Heartland Child Murders is brought to justice," Forsythe concluded.

Scroggins switched the television off. "Loves a good sound bite, doesn't he?"

"He's STILL looking at that black guy for this?" Thorne asked.

"They just took Mitchell into custody this morning, he was hiding out. They got a swab on him about an hour ago after his lawyer got done screaming. They haven't gotten the results back, but damn, Thorne, we do have a pubic hair from a black man on one of the bodies," Gilday said. "Carl Mitchell's African-American, a convicted child molester, he's still the best bet."

"Doesn't matter, he didn't do it. No black man did this. Read the file, Jethro, it's all there."

"You're sure?" Scroggins asked.

"I'm not sure, I'm fucking certain. Why do people keep asking me that? Do I look like I'm fucking around here? I wouldn't say it if I wasn't certain," Thorne grumbled.

"You know what, hotshot?" Gilday said, crossing his arms. "You haven't really said jack about the Iceman so far. Gerry and me stuck our necks out for you on Robertson and you came through, that's true, but we're here to catch the Iceman and all you're doing is pissing on the locals. You've said he ain't black and that he's in the area, but other than that, you ain't said shit."

Thorne fixed Gilday with one of his looks. "That sounds like a challenge."

"It is a challenge."

"All right," Thorne stood and went to the big map of Nebraska on the wall.

"Mitchell's a pre-teen groper, he's been caught with his hand in the candy jar more than once, in fact, the very fact that he's been arrested disqualifies him, because the guy we're looking for is much smarter than that. Mitchell is a high school dropout with the reading level of a fourth grader. The Iceman is not.

"The Iceman is a hunter, a stone-cold predator. He started up in here in North Platte a little over a year ago, right? Real slick, he operates a few months before anyone connects anything, slowly creeping east on Interstate Eighty. He picks a town, bags his kill and moves on. He stalks his victim, takes the child when he's ready for it. These are not crimes of opportunity, he takes the kids when HE decides.

"He gets into locked houses and buildings, once he even got into a locked car. He never seems to take the easy route in any of his abductions, goes for the three-pointer every time. And notice how deliberate he is about where he leaves his kills, when he does leave them; bodies have been left on playgrounds, in churches and most importantly on school grounds.

"Why? He leaves them where other children will see. So they know what he has done. This guy is smart and cold, he doesn't get rattled, does his job and enjoys his work, the cuts on the bodies smooth, clean and straight. That's not Carl Mitchell, just looking at his file you can tell that."

"Okay, say the pubic hair isn't Mitchell's," Gilday said, "but it could still belong to the Iceman, right?"

"Not a chance. He's organized, smart, knows procedure and forensics and in over twenty kills has managed to never leave any distinct physical evidence other than what he chooses ... until now? Now he leaves a pubic hair? Don't buy it. He's fucking with us. It's a classic red herring, this guy's studied up on what we do, how we do it and he threw a curveball at us. Pubic hair? That suggests sexual interaction and I don't think so. Doesn't add up, that isn't what this guy is."

"What is he?" Kane asked.

"White male, thirty to forty, well dressed and well traveled, served in the military and I'll bet he served with distinction. Likely divorced or something close to it. High IQ and educated, couple years of college. He's got a job that allows him to travel a lot, maybe a salesmen, truck driver, anything like that. I think he's a police buff, has a scanner, knows police procedure. He would probably like to be a cop," Thorne paused a moment. "He may even believe that he thinks like a cop.

"This guy looks and acts just like everyone else but inside

he's different. Inside he's not like anybody. He's a hunter, and he's after prize kills. Notice the victims here are all from stable homes, middle-class to wealthy. He targets the most protected ones, the victims that are the challenge to acquire.

"But he's smart about it, he's a sick fuck but he's not stupid. He's had these fantasies for a long time and now he's letting them loose. This is the Iceman, this is the only thing he likes to do so he's very careful about it."

"If he's this good, how can we catch him?" Scroggins asked.

"Three things for now. First thing, check the map. Mark the towns in his path that have not yet been hit. Look for a medium-sized community, five hundred to two thousand, that's what he likes best, and it's gotta have its own school, that's important. Start staking out the schoolyards, churches and playgrounds, especially at night. Have cops everywhere. He's gotta drop the next one soon."

"He doesn't always drop them."

"He'll drop this one. Put out a call for volunteers to help with this, call it a national neighborhood watch or some shit, I don't care, but take applications for it. Use these guys as eyes, but only let them have radios, no weapons, and they only watch for the Iceman in pairs. This is very important."

"Why is that?" Gilday asked.

"Because you're going to screen the volunteers. Odds are, the Iceman's going to try and involve himself in the investigation in any way that he can."

"They already got something similar to that up and running," Scroggins said. "We'll take it over, make it bigger and control it, that's a good idea."

"Screen everyone, even those that have been doing it. He'll have to involve himself if he hasn't already, he won't be able to help it," Thorne said. "Look, and look hard, at any volunteer that fits the profile and especially any ex-military."

"Jesus, do you know how many veterans there are around here?" Gilday exclaimed. "This is the Midwest, serving in the military is the thing you do if you can't play college ball."

"Shit, Jeff and I are both Gulf War vets ourselves," Scroggins said.

"Which one?" Kane asked.

"First one. The good one," Gilday answered.

"Next, release a negative profile of this guy to the media, portray him as a ticking time bomb who's definitely going to self-destruct any day now. We label him impotent, sloppy and psychotic. Kane, this is where you can get creative; he already thinks we're stupid, so let's go all the way and challenge the shit out of him. Write something up and make it sound as bad as you can. Grab him by the short and curlies, Kane."

"If he's that smart, won't he see right through it?"

"You bet, but he'll still do something about it. This guy's got a huge ego and he will not be able to let it go unanswered. The minute Carl Mitchell is cleared by the lab I want the profile on the evening news in big capital fucking letters."

"We go to the media the captain is going pitch a fit unless it's from him and his team."

"Hell yes, he's going to have kittens and I can tell you right now he's not going to want to release any misinformation, reporters hate that and the captain thinks they trust him. There's going to be a shitstorm."

"Nobody said it would be easy, boys," Thorne interrupted them. "You asked and you have received. Get your spurs jingling and jangling and move it."

"Wait," Kane said, "you said three things. What's the third thing?"

"That is the third thing," Thorne replied. "We WAIT. Wait for him. He's going to show himself to us eventually. He won't be able to resist."

CHAPTER 25

When school got out, children played in the snow on the playground as they waited for their parents. A school bus loaded up some of the kids from outlying farms, watched over warily by a beefy local cop. Darcy Mullens waited obediently just inside the school door next to her teacher Mrs. Goodwin. Darcy looked wistfully at the other kids playing in the snow, but rules were rules.

The Iceman watched Darcy from his car across the street. He glanced at the other children, but Darcy was the one that held his attention. He breathed heavily as he watched.

Barb Mullens, a red stocking cap down tight over her blonde hair, pulled up in her blue Ford Escort and honked. Darcy waved good-bye to Mrs. Goodwin, ran to her mother's car and got into the already open passenger door. Barb Mullens drove off.

The Iceman watched them go. He had an idea now.

CHAPTER 26

Thorne sat with his feet up on his desk, staring at his chessboard, supplanting that with an occasional glance out the window where fat snowflakes fell heavily in the night. Kane approached his desk, file in hand, and sat down next to him. Thorne had a faraway look in his eye, one that grabbed hold of him on rare occasions.

Kane had noticed that Thorne was almost sociable when he got this look. She didn't associate it with the music he had currently playing on his CD player, not even knowing who Charlie "Bird" Parker was.

"Here's the release, I sent a copy to Norm and everyone; what do you think?" Kane handed him her creation. Thorne gave it a quick read.

"Good. This should piss him off; you all but said he has a tiny dick. There may be hope for you yet."

"Jeff and Gerry got this into the pipeline and everything else that you said is rolling forward. Anything else we can do?" Kane asked.

"Just wait," Thorne said absently.

"Anything else we can do besides that?"

"Nothing else we can do at this point."

Kane fidgeted for a moment. "I hate waiting."

"I don't know anybody that really likes it," Thorne said. "Ever watch the nature channel? Only decent thing on television these days. I love that shit, I really love watching the polar bears hunt, you ever see that? A polar bear will sit watching a hole in the ice for hours until finally a seal pops its head up for a half a second to catch a breath of air and zip-zip, BING! Polar bear's got himself a seal sandwich."

"So you're certain that he will pop his head up?" Kane asked.

"Remember rule number one. I am always right."

"I don't like that story. I like seals."

"Too bad, you want to be a profiler, you're going to have to learn to like polar bears."

"Why does the Iceman do what he does?"

"You tell me," Thorne made a move on his board.

"Sex thing?"

"What is he, Kane? WHAT does he do?"

"He's a hunter."

"And why do hunters hunt?"

"Well, for sport."

"Why else?"

"For ..." It suddenly dawned on her and Kane gawked at Thorne, open-mouthed.

"That's right," Thorne said. "They do. And sometimes they do it for both of those reasons, like our boy here."

"But how do you know ..."

"Why else do we only find just pieces of victims, here and there? He's careful, he doesn't want us know, at least not yet, but that's exactly what he's doing. Look at the pictures, look at how the bodies have been cut, do you think that's accidental? Think about it. It's the only explanation."

"Why haven't you said anything to anyone else about this?"

"I haven't even really said it to you. You came up with this on your own. But to answer your question: Timing, Kane. All in the timing."

"Oh my God. So that's why?"

"That's part of why. Not the whole part of why, but a big part. When we can break down the rest of the why, then we'll know where and who and we'll be there before he cracks open the A-1 sauce."

Kane was silent for a moment. "I've seen a lot of things, bad things, working DC Homicide isn't Disneyland, but … I don't know how some people can do the things they can do."

"You're on that HOW thing again. Come on, Kane, there are three or four billion people on this planet. They all do weird shit and there's no real explanation for it. I don't understand the attraction rollerblading holds for people, or how anyone can listen to gangsta rap, but it happens. It's there, it happens. People do it.

"No rhyme or reason other than that the shit that people do is the shit that people do. Learn it, live it and know it. One of the few constants in life, Kane," Thorne selected a rook on his chessboard and moved it, "is that shit happens."

Kane had to think about that for a couple of minutes. "Thorne, do you believe in life after death?"

"I'm still not sure about life before death."

"There's got to be a reason for things like this. I have to believe that."

"That's all those bullshit TV shows speaking for you. All right, Kane," Thorne lowered his feet and rubbed his hands together.

"Let's do a little exercise. Picture in your mind a young boy, one with no real friends, no brothers or sisters, one whose parents alternately ignore and abuse. Got the picture?

Okay, now you know what this little boy's doing? He's killing bugs. In his spare time he's killing all the bugs he can, mashing caterpillars, pulling legs off of grasshoppers, digging up anthills and going to war with them.

"He kills bugs all the time. He's real creative about it too, douses them with glue and lighter fluid and anything else he can get his hands on. He gets real good at it. Now. Tell me. Why does he do that?"

"Killing bugs gives him a sense of power in his life," Kane replied, her eyes lighting up. "He lives a life which is subject to the whims of others, one where he's not in control, he doesn't get a choice in what happens. Killing bugs gives him a chance to be in control, the ability to choose who lives, who doesn't. Right?"

"Wrong. That's the television answer. The real answer: He just likes killing bugs. That's just what he is, a bug killer. He does it because he likes it and that's what he is. Maybe he'll grow up and become a bug exterminator, maybe he'll move up the killing chain from bugs to animals to people.

"One we don't concern ourselves with, the other we do. But it doesn't change what he is and always will be, a killer," Thorne leaned back and put his feet back up on his desk. "And our job is to be able to know a killer when we see him, bug, animal or otherwise."

"But ..."

"No buts. You want to know how I do what I do, there it is."

Forsythe suddenly appeared in their line of vision, very red in the face. He stomped over to the federal officers and, with one swipe of a meaty paw, knocked Thorne's feet off the table where they were resting comfortably.

"What the fuck do you think you are doing? Who the fuck do you think you are? You don't dictate policy HERE, you don't delegate actions or tell ANYONE on this task force

WHAT TO DO!" Forsythe was screaming now, spittle flying from his mouth.

Heads from nearby desks popped up to watch and listen to the fireworks. Thorne simply stared at Forsythe impassively.

"Now, you may have pulled a slick trick or two outa your ass, you MAY have done that, but I don't care what you think you've accomplished," Forsythe continued. "I'm in charge of this operation here. Either accept that or get the fuck OUT! If I have to go to the governor to make that clear to you, I will do that. I am THE BOSS! And do you know what that means? It means you DON'T DO ANYTHING WITHOUT CHECKING WITH ME FIRST!

"Are we clear on this? You don't talk to anyone, you don't go anywhere, you don't crack a fart without asking me for permission first. This 'media profile release' SHIT, it's not happening. You, interrogating another suspect, not happening. You, going to another crime scene, not happening. You, firing your weapon at anyone ELSE, not fucking happening. From now on, you don't do ANYTHING except read and write reports and if you have ANY recommendations, you make them to ME and ONLY me. Now then. If either of you have a problem with that, then I suggest you get your asses back to Washington or wherever it is you came from! Any questions? Good!"

Forsythe wheeled and stalked off, still cursing under his breath. Thorne turned to Kane, a thoughtful look on his face.

"Case in point," Thorne said. "I'll be right back."

Thorne casually got to his feet and walked after Forsythe.

CHAPTER 27

Forsythe sat on the toilet in a stall in the men's room, moved his bowels and read the newspaper. This was his ritual, three times a day he sat, whether he needed to or not, here on the throne where every man was king and hoped for delivery. In addition to regular sitting was an awful orange-flavored fiber drink his wife made him drink every morning and evening. Men his age had to pay attention to their bowels, among other things, was the wife's constant refrain.

The door to the men's room opened and closed. Forsythe paid no attention to it, engrossed in his paper and the loud trumpeting noises that emitted from his posterior, signaling fiber-coated success.

Footsteps echoed off the bathroom walls. They stopped directly in front of Forsythe's stall. This got Forsythe's attention. He lowered the paper and looked down at the bottom of his stall door. A pair of shoes faced his stall. The right shoe tapped calmly.

"Who's fucking around out there?" Forsythe growled, feeling his blood pressure begin to rise yet again.

Thorne suddenly kicked the door open and leaped into the stall. He grabbed Forsythe by his hair and tie and dragged him out of the toilet stall. He propelled Forsythe, struggling to pull up his pants, right into the bathroom wall.

The big man hit his head hard on the wall. Thorne grabbed Forsythe again, turned him around and threw him right back into the toilet stall where he was previously sitting. Forsythe hit the toilet, slipped and fell to the floor next to it.

Thorne, chewing gum, calmly grabbed Forsythe by the hair, lifted his head up and very deliberately shoved his face into the just-used toilet bowl. Forsythe bellowed and thrashed but, despite his weight and size advantage, was helpless in Thorne's grip.

Thorne casually dunked Forsythe's head into the used toilet once, twice, three times and then flushed the toilet on his face. Thorne hauled Forsythe up to his feet and tossed him out of the stall yet again. Forsythe slipped and fell to the floor, his pants still only as high as his knees. Bracing his hands on the floor and panting, Forsythe tried to get up.

Thorne kicked Forsythe in the gut hard. All the wind went right out of Forsythe. Forsythe tried to raise himself once more, bracing his arms yet again. Thorne calmly kicked Forsythe's hand out from under him before he could do so. Forsythe fell heavily onto the floor on his face. He lay there on his chest, breathing heavily.

Thorne leaned down, grabbed one of Forsythe's shoulders and flipped him over onto his back. Forsythe looked up at Thorne from the floor like a whipped puppy.

"We're having a serious disagreement here," Thorne said, still calm. "For the record, I'll state my case. YOU. Do NOT … get in my WAY … at any point in time. EVER. Other than that, I don't care what you do. Have I made myself clear?"

Forsythe, still breathing heavily, closed his eyes and nodded.

"Good. I don't want to have to have this conversation again," Thorne checked his look in the mirror, adjusted his tie and ran his fingers through his hair.

"I'm hungry," Thorne said. "You know any good restaurants? I'm hungry for Italian food. Can you even get decent Italian in Nebraska?"

Forsythe swallowed and coughed, still on his back. "Pepe's. On Avenue B and Twelfth. It's not too bad."

"Thanks," Thorne said, "I appreciate it."

Thorne left the bathroom. Forsythe stayed exactly where he was on the floor.

As Thorne strolled out of the men's room, a couple of uniformed men stood outside the door cautiously, hands on weapons, unsure what to do about the racket that had come from the bathroom. Hairston stared at Thorne for a moment before entering the john with a worried look on his face.

"Careful in there, floor's wet and a little slippery," Thorne said as Hairston hurried by him. "I think someone may have fallen." Kane stood a few feet away, eyebrow raised.

"Kane! Wanna get some chow? I'm starving, come on," Thorne turned to Johnson, sitting wide-eyed at his desk. "Johnson! I'm going for Italian, give me a car."

"Well, uh," Johnson stuttered, "I don't know if …"

"Johnson," Thorne glared at him, "don't make me come over there."

Johnson quickly tossed a set of car keys to Thorne, who caught them gracefully. "Blue four-door sedan, right out front," Johnson said.

"Good man. Let's roll, Kane, come on come on," Thorne grabbed his coat and headed for the door. Forsythe came out of the men's room carefully, supported by Hairston and another uniformed cop.

"I'm all right, I slipped," Forsythe said. "It's nothing, it happens. I'm all right."

Kane grabbed her coat and hurried after Thorne.

CHAPTER 28

"**W**hat was that about?" Kane asked after she caught up to Thorne outside on the steps of headquarters.

"What was what about?" Thorne struggled with his coat. It was completely dark out now and snow fell heavily, causing Thorne much frustration as he tramped toward the parked cars.

"You, Forsythe, bathroom, the noise, the shouting, what do you think?"

"Attitude adjustment," Thorne said. "Does it ever stop snowing here?"

Thorne finally found the blue four-door sedan parked between two patrol cars and went to the driver's side. Kane walked around to the passenger side, glanced across the street and went real still when something caught her eye.

"Thorne," Kane said, quiet.

"What?" Thorne fumbled with the car keys, looked up and followed her gaze.

Across the street, a man stood under a streetlight. He wore a black ski mask over his face and in his arms held a small figure wrapped in a white sheet. He gently lowered the tiny figure to the ground, arranging it on the ground just so, and then straightened back up to his full height. He stared at Thorne and Kane as heavy snow fell between them.

"It's him," Thorne said, carefully reaching for his weapon.

The air around the two of them suddenly exploded as the Iceman opened fire on them before they could react. Bullets crashed into the parked cars and Thorne and Kane hit the deck behind the sedan, diving out of the way. The sedan's windshield collapsed from the gunfire. The night went silent once again.

Weapons drawn, they poked their heads up over a car. The Iceman was still standing there, watching them, weapon now at his side. The Iceman turned and ran down the street into the falling snow and darkness. Thorne and Kane leaped up to follow, Thorne slipping a little. Kane detoured toward the small body wrapped in white.

"Leave her, she's gone!" Thorne yelled. "Stay with him!"

The Iceman turned a corner a block ahead of them, staying in the center of the suburban city street. Thorne beat ass down the road after him, Kane not far behind. Cops poured out of headquarters, weapons drawn, trying to figure out what the hell just happened. They arrived just in time to see Kane disappear into the snowstorm.

Thorne made the first turn in time to see the Iceman take another turn down another street, barely seen in the blowing snow. Thorne pushed himself even harder, having trouble getting traction in his shoes. He came to the second corner but slipped and fell down hard on his rear while making the turn. Looking up, Thorne could see the Iceman make a left turn down yet another street a block away. Thorne aimed his weapon but before he could fire, the Iceman was gone from view.

Kane, running fast, passed Thorne as he struggled to rise.

"He took a left, he took a fucking left!" Thorne yelled.

Kane nodded and streaked past him, falling into the easy rhythm she used every morning at home on her treadmill where she did five miles a day. Kane ran confident, knowing that she was fully capable of running hard for over an hour, even in her boots in the snow. She reached the next street down and turned left.

In the distance she could just barely see the shadow of the Iceman. He wasn't going to outrun her. She would run him into the ground first. Kane picked up her pace. Thorne got to his feet and managed to follow Kane for a few feet before slipping again and falling heavily on the icy street.

"Goddamn these fucking shoes!" Thorne yelled.

Thorne stood back up just in time to see Kane completely disappear into the snowy night. Thorne was only able to take a few steps before falling on his ass yet again.

"Fuck! Fuck the snow and ice, fuck!" Thorne cursed up at the sky.

Kane ran hard, pushing her body way up past her usual limits. The Iceman ran ahead of her, a little over a block away. The street they were on took them to the edge of the city. Snow fell even heavier in the night and blurred visibility to almost nothing. The Iceman turned behind to check his pursuer's progress. He raised his weapon and fired at Kane. She could hear the bullet whiz over her head. Still she ran.

The Iceman reached the edge of town and the railroad freight station. He slipped through a large chained gate leading to the grounds of the railroad freight yard. Kane doubled her speed, reached the gate and slipped under the chain herself. Kane spotted the Iceman running towards a group of large metal shipping containers. She lost sight of him as he ducked into the shadows between two of the containers.

Kane slowed when she came to the virtual maze of railroad storage containers that the Iceman had disappeared into. Her breath came out in frosty plumes, very fast and heavy, and she forced herself to take her time now. Kane walked very cautiously, her weapon out in front her, hunting.

Thorne, a few blocks away, ran a bit more carefully now, trying to track them from their prints in the snow before they got completely filled in. Sirens wailed from a distance.

Kane carefully followed the Iceman's tracks in the snow past several metal containers. She stopped between two of them and listened. The only sound that could be heard was the howling wind and her breathing. There was very little light to see by.

The Iceman's tracks continued onward, past the next metal container and into the darkness on the other side of the maze. Kane slowly inched forward, preparing herself for what might be around the corner.

A gloved hand came out of the shadows next to Kane and grabbed her gun hand. The Iceman twisted her arm and leveraged her right into the side of the metal container. Kane slammed into it hard and dropped her gun into the snow.

Kane aimed a kick at the Iceman but he blocked it and countered with a left hook to her jaw that stunned her. The Iceman backhanded Kane and she went down, face first, bleeding from the mouth, nearly unconscious.

The Iceman pulled his weapon out from his belt and slowly walked around Kane with it pointed at her. Kane's head spun and she could barely see as she struggled to get up on her hands and knees. Nausea took over and she collapsed. The Iceman leaned down and pressed his firearm right into the back of her head. With his other hand he rolled Kane onto her back. His weapon right under her chin, he eased the hammer back, and prepared to fire.

But he didn't.

Instead, with his free hand, the Iceman delicately brushed

hair and snow off of Kane's face and out of her eyes. Kane slowly opened her eyes, still groggy, and saw the Iceman leaning over her with his hand on her face. The Iceman slowly stood, took a step back, and as she looked at him he disappeared into the night. Kane closed her eyes.

When she next opened her eyes, Thorne stood over her much in the same way the Iceman had. Thorne scooped her up and carried her out of there, walking very carefully so as not to slip.

CHAPTER 29

"We've gone over every inch of the freight yard. We've got a couple partial footprints, a bunch of fibers, one of which hopefully belongs to our man, but other than that nothing else," Scroggins said as he entered the observation room of the County Coroner. "Is that the Frederickson girl?"

"Who else?" Thorne asked. "Where were the fibers found?"

Forsythe and Hairston stood silent behind Thorne as they all watched the autopsy in progress. A coroner examined the body of Wendy Frederickson on the other side of the window, his assistants and Gilday close by. Gilday looked ill. Thorne held a note in his hand, wrapped in a clear plastic baggie.

"All over the place, but we did get one good one from the chain on the gate, we're hoping it's his."

"The weapon?"

"Recovered the bullets, they're down at the lab now, the techies can definitely link it to the weapon if we can find the gun, but without the weapon they're not sure. A forty-five."

"Forty-five?" Thorne turned his head. "Who carries a forty-five anymore?"

"Well," Scroggins began.

"Military police, that's who," Thorne interrupted him. "Soldiers carry forty-five sidearms."

"Yeah, I was afraid you'd say that."

Gilday entered from the exam room.

"Cause of death, suffocation," Gilday said. "Didn't cut this one, didn't do anything to her as far as the doc can tell except smother her with a pillow. Doc said she's been dead awhile, probably soon after her abduction, but he won't be able to get an exact time of death. Decomposition has been slowed considerably, so the body was either kept outside or in a freezer after death.

"Couple of hair and fibers unaccounted for, some of the fibers probably came from the pillow used and if we find the pillow he can match the fibers to it. There are no finger-prints. They did get another pubic hair off the body. It's preliminary but the doc says it looks like it matches the hair that we found on the last girl."

"Another pubic hair and it's African-American?" Hairston asked.

"That's what the man said."

"And it definitely leaves Carl Mitchell out of it, he's been in lock-up this whole time," Scroggins said. "This is the first time he didn't cut, why didn't he cut her this time?"

Thorne held up the note in the baggie.

"Doc told me there was a note left on the body, that's it?" Gilday asked.

Thorne nodded and stared at the body of the young girl on the other side of the glass. Everyone looked at each other for a moment. Gilday cleared his throat.

"You going to tell us what's on the note or not?" he asked finally.

"What's mine is yours, therefore what's yours is mine. I left a ripe one whole for you, so enjoy, enjoy, she has such lovely eyes," Thorne read from the letter. "Before I'm done I will take from you what you most prize."

"What the hell does that mean?" Scroggins asked. "Now he's writing poetry? Does that mean anything to anyone?"

"It means he watches too much fucking television, that's what it means," Thorne grunted.

"It's a challenge," Hairston said. "He's challenging you."

Everyone looked at Hairston, who grew a little uncomfortable.

"You're right, Norman," Thorne said. "That's exactly what it is. A challenge. That's why he came right to Task Force Headquarters to drop the body. That's why he waited for us almost on our fucking steps and threw shots at us; he thinks we're shit and he's challenging us. To be even more specific, he's challenging me."

"How do you know that?" Scroggins asked.

"Has he taken a shot at any of you?"

"Is Emma all right?" Gilday asked.

"She'll live, bumped her head running in the dark. Now this," Thorne held up the note, "I want this fucking scrutinized, up and down, backwards and forwards. It came from a word processor or a computer printer. I want to know what kind, what brand, I want everything. Clear?"

Thorne handed the note to Hairston, who looked to Forsythe for confirmation. Forsythe nodded. Scroggins and Gilday exchanged a look.

"Scroggins, I want you to hit the armory at every Military and National Guard base within two hundred square miles, you know what I'm looking for, young man, go after it. Gilday, get the uniformed teams working with the neighborhood watch in place and ready. Stay especially salty, he's going snatch somebody quick and it's going to be someone in this area. Forsythe!"

"What?" Forsythe was startled.

"Make a statement to the press, I don't care what, something smooth and comforting and make sure you encourage people to join the neighborhood watch. Get pictures of yourself comforting the girl's parents in the papers and on the news.

"Let people know they are never to leave their children alone at any time. This guy is going to make a move on a girl sometime in the next twenty-four hours, he's hungry, he's coming this way and he won't wait."

"Maybe we should cancel school? Some parents have been keeping their kids home already," Forsythe asked.

"It won't wash for everyone, if both parents work, then the kids are home alone and vulnerable. He hits at home," Hairston said. "School is actually safer, we have uniforms stationed at every elementary school in the state."

"Give parents the option of keeping them home, but never left alone at anytime," Thorne said. "Make sure everyone in this state understands, no child should be left unattended. He wants a challenge, that's what he's going to get. That's it, get going."

Thorne turned his gaze back to the young girl's body lying on the table on the other side of the glass. He made himself watch the entire autopsy from start to finish.

CHAPTER 30

Kane sat on an exam table in Emergency with an icepack to the side of her head. Her left eye was black and her lower lip swollen. Thorne pulled back the curtains with an angry yank, the autopsy still fresh in his mind. He was behind the curve and he didn't like it.

"How's it look?" Kane asked.

Thorne tilted her head back for a look. "It's an improvement. What's the prognosis?"

"No stitches, pounding headache. Extreme embarrassment. That's twice you've saved my life."

"Yeah," Thorne sat opposite her, "and I don't even like you."

"Do you really not like me?"

"I really don't like you."

"Nice boots, by the way."

Thorne wore new boots, hiking boots with a thick, heavy tread.

"I like them. Good traction. Adaptability, very important, Kane. Polar bears are very adaptable."

"You were right about him coming to us."

"Of course I was right," Thorne said. "Why do I have to keep reminding everyone?"

"The Frederickson girl? She's dead?"

"She's dead. That brings his total to twenty."

"Twenty little girls. And I was close enough to smell him and I fucking let him get away."

"Yes. He got away from both of us."

"He's like a ghost or something."

"No, he's not. He's got different appetites than we do, but other than that he's human, he breathes, he bleeds and he can and will die. He has to sit in order to shit, just like everybody else."

"Thorne," Kane said after a moment, "do you believe in good and evil?"

"No."

"What do you believe in?"

"Brains. Balls. Inspiration and imagination. Observable fact. Old school arithmetic. Classic jazz. Capital punishment. Breakfast at any hour of the day. Non-fat yogurt."

"Anything else?"

"Winning."

"Why did the Iceman come after us?"

"He thinks he's the hero of the picture."

"Hero of what?" Kane asked.

"The picture in his head," Thorne stood to leave. "In the movie running in his head, he's the hero, he's the star."

"In his mind he's the hero and we're the bad guys?"

"That's what he thinks. Little does he realize, I'm the name above the title, I get top billing, I'm the fucking STAR of this show."

CHAPTER 31

Snow fell, though not as heavy as earlier. School let out and children played on the playground while waiting for their parents. A beefy uniformed policeman stood guard at the entrance of the school and another watched the playground with eagle eyes.

Darcy Mullens waited just inside her school door, looking wistfully yet again as the other kids played in the snow. Mrs. Goodwin stood nearby, keeping a close eye on all her charges. A car honked.

"There's your mother, honey," Mrs. Goodwin said. "Have a good weekend."

"Bye, Mrs. Goodwin."

Barb Mullens, behind the wheel of her blue Ford Escort in her standard red stocking cap, reached over and opened the passenger door for Darcy. She honked again. Darcy waved good-bye to her friends and then ran to her mother's car, got in and shut the car door quickly. They drove off.

Mrs. Goodwin found herself distracted by a fight between two children on the playground. After breaking it up and scolding the youngsters for their lack of holiday goodwill, she heard a familiar car horn honk.

Barb Mullens's blue Ford Escort again parked and waiting in the bus zone. Mrs. Goodwin walked over to the car, confused and curious. Barb Mullens, in her red stocking cap, rolled her window down.

"Hello, Mrs. Mullens, did you forget ..." Mrs. Goodwin stopped short.

She saw that Barb Mullens was sitting in her car alone.

"Sorry I'm late, Mrs. Goodwin, I had a flat tire," Barb Mullens said. "Where's Darcy?"

* * *

IN A BLUE FORD ESCORT very similar to the one owned by Barb Mullens, her daughter Darcy looked up in confusion at the person driving the vehicle.

A red stocking cap and a blonde wig landed on the car seat next to Darcy.

Darcy looked at the wig and then back up at the Iceman, who whistled a Christmas tune as he drove them both towards destination unknown.

"Where's my Mommy?" Darcy asked, more than a little scared.

CHAPTER 32

An hour later, Thorne wandered the elementary school hallway. Uniformed policeman and CSU technicians were everywhere, inside and out, interviewing teachers, frightened children and custodial staff. News vans clustered just beyond the patrol cars outside. Thorne leaned against a locker as Kane approached him.

"So somebody, dressed like her mother," Thorne began, "in a car just like her mother's, drives up, picks the kid up and nobody notices that it's not the kid's mother?"

"That's the situation," Kane replied. "The teacher swears that whoever it was looked just like the mother. Maybe it's been a woman we've been after this whole time."

"No. The Iceman is male, not female, don't even go there," Thorne said.

"Women snatch children all the time, thinking they belong to them, thinking …"

"You're making noise, Kane. It's a man that snatched this kid. It was a man that shot at us, it was a man that we chased through a blizzard and it was a man that knocked you on your ass."

"Maybe it's a couple, a man and woman, working together, like that case in Canada," Kane said.

"No, Kane," Thorne cut her off, "stop making noise and listen to the music. This is one guy, one smart and ballsy fucking guy with an agenda."

"He's getting close; this is what, twenty miles from headquarters?" Kane said. "Norman Hairston called me. They got the lab back on the pubic hair. The hair on both bodies was a match, they came from the same person. DNA does not match Carl Mitchell, which is hardly surprising since he was in jail when we were getting shot at by the Iceman."

"And also because I said he didn't do it," Thorne said.

"But what was surprising is that they did get a DNA match on it, they got a name, somebody already in the system," Kane said.

"Let me guess. Hair matched that of a man who is already dead."

"How did you know that?"

"Because if the Iceman had plucked a few pubes from a live man, said live man just might remember him. I would. Get on with it, Kane."

"Well, you're right. The hair came from Trent Boyd, African-American, resident of Omaha, Nebraska, killed in a traffic accident five months ago. They're getting an order from the judge to exhume the body, verify that Boyd is indeed dead as the death certificate says he is."

"Waste of time, he's definitely dead and someone plucked his pubes. Check the mortuary where Boyd was interred, it'll be a dead end but do it anyway, find the cop who processed the accident scene, the paramedics that drove the ambulance, I want it all. Also, backtrack his friends, family and acquaintances and find out if Mr. Boyd served in the military and if there's anyone in the area that served with him."

"So the Iceman planted it, then, to fuck with us?"

"Now you're singing, Kane. This isn't a case that's going to be closed by forensics. This guy lives for fuckery. Anything else?"

"Jesus Fucking Christ!" Scroggins entered the hallway, furious. "Darcy Mullens. I can't believe this is happening here of all places!"

"Why not here?" Thorne asked.

"I live here! I grew up in this town."

"You grew up here?" Kane asked.

"Denton, Nebraska, population eight hundred nine. Three churches, two bars and one school. I went to school here, I played football here, I've lived here my whole fucking life, three miles right outside of town. Fuck!" Scroggins punched one of the lockers.

Gilday joined them.

"We're doing a run on all the blue Ford Escorts in the county, but it'll take awhile. I can't believe this. Gerry, you talk to Barb yet?"

"No, I didn't, and I seriously doubt she wants to talk to me," Scroggins glared at Gilday.

"Come on, man, don't be that way."

"Who's Barb?" Thorne asked.

"Barb Mullens," Kane replied. "Darcy's mother."

"We know Barb, we all went to school together," Gilday said.

"You live here too?" Kane asked.

"I grew up here, I moved to Lincoln when my folks passed away, ten years or so ago," Gilday replied. "This building here used to hold all twelve grades, but the school district expanded and now this building is just the elementary school, the junior high and high school students take the bus to Gowrie."

"Where's the mother now?" Thorne asked.

"At the hospital under sedation. The father, Chad Mullens, is there with her now."

"Here's a picture of the girl," Kane handed a school photo to Thorne. "Darcy Mullens, age seven, blonde hair and blue eyes."

"Blue eyes?" Thorne furrowed his brow.

"Just like her ma," Gilday said.

"Blue eyes," Thorne repeated.

"How well do you know the parents?" Kane asked.

"Barb, Gerry and I were all in the same class together. Chad went to school here too, he was two years ahead of us," Gilday replied. "But it's no secret that Gerry knows Barb a lot better than I do."

"You fucking asshole," Scroggins pushed Gilday hard against the lockers.

"What's your problem, it's the truth, isn't it?" Gilday said, shocked into anger and pushed Scroggins back. Scroggins grabbed Gilday by the jacket, cursing.

Kane got between the two and separated them. "Hey! Hey! Cut the shit!" The two men glared at each other, breathing heavily.

Uniformed personnel poked their heads out of different rooms to see what was going on. Thorne watched the whole drama impassively.

"Look, fellas," Kane said after a moment, "we're all under pressure here. Let's just take it easy."

"Come on, man, it's not like it's not gonna come out," Gilday said.

"Jeff, why don't you go puke or something," Scroggins replied, his neck red with anger. "Isn't that what you usually do at a crime scene?"

Scroggins stalked off.

"What was that all about?" Kane demanded.

"Barb and Gerry went out together in high school, three years," Gilday sighed. "She dear-Johned him while we were in the service, ended up marrying Chad Mullens. They don't even talk to each other even though they live in the same town. He's touchy about it and I should've known better."

"So he had a personal connection with the victim?"

"Shit of course, but so did I, we've known her and Chad our whole lives. There isn't anyone in town Gerry doesn't have a personal connection to in some way. There are at least four or five other kids in the same class whose mother is someone Gerry or I dated at least once at some point before they got hitched. It's a small town. This is hitting too fucking close to home, man."

Kane looked at Thorne.

"Don't look at each other like that, don't fucking ... Gerry is a stand-up fucking guy."

"Why this town?" Thorne asked. "Why here, why now?"

"Is he fucking with members of the task force?" Kane asked him. "Is he deliberately targeting those close to the people that are working on his case?"

"He deliberately targeted us last night, didn't he?" Thorne replied.

"What's mine is yours, and yours is mine," Kane repeated. "I will take away what you most prize."

"Jesus Christ," Gilday said. "You think he's gonna start hitting us where we live? I know a bunch of guys on this case that have kids about this age, if he's going to start doing that there's gonna be a lot of fucking suspects shot while trying to escape."

"You think that's what going on, Thorne?" Kane asked.

"Maybe. I don't know yet," Thorne replied, thinking.

"What about Forsythe, does he have daughters?" Kane asked.

"He does, but they're too old."

"Why the eyes?" Thorne asked them both.

"What?" Kane said.

"Why lovely eyes? Who says that? Why say that? Why put that in the note? Gilday! The Frederickson girl," Thorne said.

"What about her?"

"Did they check her entire body for fingerprints?" Thorne asked.

"Far as I know the man checked everything," Gilday replied.

"Even the eyeballs themselves?"

"I don't know," Gilday admitted.

"Then go find out. Find out now," Thorne said.

CHAPTER 33

Later that night Thorne contemplated his chessboard while Thelonious Monk played softly on the CD player next to him. Not far from him, Gilday sat at a desk and tapped away on a computer while talking into a phone cradled on his neck. A television with the volume muted nearby broadcast the news, which featured photos of Darcy Mullens. Kane approached Thorne from the other side of the room.

"Found the car, ten miles outside of town, dumped. Clean so far, no prints, nothing," she said. "It was reported stolen from Cedar City yesterday."

Thorne glanced up and then looked past her. Kane followed his gaze. Scroggins stood behind her, watching the television screen. Barb and Chad Mullens pleaded silently onscreen into microphones. Both were crying. Scroggins walked over and took a seat next to Thorne.

"It's probably too late for Darcy, isn't it?" Scroggins asked him.

"Probably. Not positively, but probably."

"Thorne," Scroggins said after a moment, "I want this pig-fucking Iceman, I want him like I've never wanted anything in my entire life, are you listening to me? No easy mental time, no jail time, I want him screaming and dead. Now, I'm going to ask you a question and I don't want one of your smart-ass federal bullshit answers. I want to know, can you catch this cocksucker or not?"

"I can catch him. I will catch him."

"I got your word on that?"

"You got my word."

Scroggins looked at Thorne for a moment and then held out his hand to shake. Thorne reluctantly surrendered to another bone-crusher. Scroggins stood and walked over to Gilday, who still had the phone to his ear.

"Hey, Jeff?" Scroggins said quietly.

"Yeah?" Gilday put his hand over the receiver.

"About, you know, earlier …"

"Gerry, it's nothing, forget about it."

"I just wanna say …"

"We're best friends. You don't have to say anything."

"I'm sorry, that's all," Scroggins held out his hand.

Gilday gripped his partner's fist until the knuckles went white. Thorne shook his head at this display and went back to his game.

Forsythe and Hairston joined the group. Hairston handed a report to Thorne. Kane noticed that Forsythe never looked directly at Thorne anymore, preferring to watch him from the corner of his eyes now whenever possible.

"Report on the note left on the body," Hairston said. "No prints, but it's been determined that it was printed by an Epson Stylus 700, a pretty common computer printer. If we can find the printer, we'll be able to match it."

"In other words, not much help at all," Thorne said.

"Basically," Hairston said, glancing at his silent boss. "So Agent Thorne, what do you recommend we do next?"

Thorne thought about that for a moment.

"Well," he began.

"What!" Gilday interrupted, shouting into the telephone. "Are you positive? Hell yeah, run it! Run it right now, I'll network with you!" Gilday slammed the phone down and looked at everyone.

"What is it?" Kane asked.

"We got a partial, we got a fucking partial!"

Gilday turned his computer screen toward everyone so they could see the large picture of a fingerprint on it. The program ran quickly, comparing the print with other prints in its memory.

"You got a print?" Forsythe bulled his way over to the desk.

"Off of the Frederickson's girl left eyeball; it's only a partial thumb print, but it's a good one we can run. He touched her eyes, just like Thorne said, with his bare fingers. It's going through VICAP and CODIS now, if he's ever been arrested or printed for anything for any reason, we'll know it in seconds!" Gilday hunched over the computer, excited, as everyone except Thorne crowded him.

"Run it through the state and federal database as well. If he's employed as we are, it'll flag," Thorne said. This possibility quieted the group.

Thorne stared at his chessboard, concentrating for a moment, and then looked up at the map of Nebraska on the wall. The computer beeped.

"Oh my God. We got a hit. We got him!" Gilday said. "Bart McNeil."

"Bart fucking McNeil?" Scroggins asked. "I know him, I once arrested him for beating the shit out of his wife!"

"I know him too, I busted him for DUI once. Bart McNeil, forty-five, ex-Marine, divorced now, big drinking problem," Gilday read information on the screen. "Lives in Crete, that's only ten miles away from Denton. Get this, he's taken the cop test three times and failed, he's a volunteer on the neighborhood watch and he drives a Schwann's Ice Cream delivery truck; his route covers half the state of Nebraska."

"Ice cream. Iceman," Kane said.

Everyone turned to look at Thorne, who stared at the map on the wall. Thorne, feeling everyone's gaze, finally stirred from his funk.

"How soon can you get a warrant?" Thorne asked Forsythe.

"I can get one five minutes ago."

After a moment, Thorne sighed. "All right, Captain. Go get him."

Forsythe jolted into action, Hairston close behind as usual. "Norm, call the judge and wake his ass up! Bill, get the SWAT boys geared up, we're moving and we're moving right now! Let's go!"

Men and women in uniform all over headquarters were galvanized into movement. Scroggins and Gilday checked their weapons and grabbed their jackets. Thorne stood and stopped them with a gesture.

"You two going in with them?" he asked.

"Hell yes!" Scroggins replied.

"Then do me a favor."

"What's that?" Gilday asked.

"Take him alive. I want him to get the needle, so take him alive, all right?"

Gilday nodded after a moment. Scroggins looked hard at Thorne, not saying anything. The two men hurried off. Kane grabbed her jacket, watching Thorne, who sat down at Gilday's computer and calmly printed out the file on Bart McNeil.

"Are you coming?" Kane asked.

"I am definitely coming," he replied.

CHAPTER 34

L ess than an hour later, SWAT policemen in riot gear quietly surrounded the house of Bart McNeil. Crete was, if anything, an even smaller town than Denton. The house was dark and rundown, with untrimmed hedges and a driveway covered in snow that hadn't been shoveled at all, only driven over. A Schwann's Ice Cream truck sat in the drive. A light was on somewhere deep in the house.

Hairston drove an unmarked police van with its lights off down the street and parked a half a block away. Forsythe turned to Gilday and Scroggins, geared up and heavily armed, sitting behind him. Kane and Thorne sat in the back behind everyone.

"He hasn't been to work in a couple days, called in sick," Forsythe said. "His machine is picking up, but he's probably screening calls. His truck is in the driveway. Unless he's walking, he's in there. Which one of you knows him better?"

"Shit, I don't know. He's about to wish he didn't know me at all. Jeff?" Scroggins said, adjusting his headset mike.

"I've run into him enough he knows my name."

"Are we going in?" Kane asked.

"Not a chance," Forsythe said, "this scumfucker is OUR bust."

"Cops first, fibbies second," Scroggins said.

"But the girl might still be alive in there …"

"Cops take the door, Kane, we've been shot at enough," Thorne said.

"It's our job, Emma. You all pointed us at him, we go get him," Gilday added.

Forsythe spoke into the radio on his shoulder. "Command One to all teams, secure perimeter, key headset twice when in position. Wait for my go, repeat, wait for my go."

"Scroggins," Thorne put his hand on Scroggins's shoulder, leaned forward and spoke into his ear. Gilday listened in.

"What?"

"If you run in there now and shoot him right in the face, he won't ever know that you caught him, he won't know you won, he won't even know that he's dead," Thorne said. "That's not what you want, you get me?

"You want to hear dead and screaming, you should see these fuckers once we get them strapped on the gurney and shove the needle into their arm. They scream, they beg, they piss their pants like a baby. I've seen it, more than once, and it's very fulfilling. It's much more satisfying than just blowing him away, you hear me?"

"Takes too long, though, don't it?" Scroggins said quietly.

"Takes awhile but it's totally worth it. Trust me, I know what I'm talking about. I wouldn't start lying to spare your feelings at this point, would I?"

Scroggins and Gilday glanced at each other.

"Hell, Thorne, we all know what a tactful bastard you are," Gilday said.

"No easy mental time, right?" Scroggins asked Thorne.

"No easy mental time. He'll get the needle, quicker than you can say Timothy McVeigh. No judge or jury has patience for a killer of children. They'll put him on the gurney. Just bring him back alive, gentlemen, if you can, alive."

"Okay," Forsythe turned back to them. "Let's do this."

"Ready?" Gilday asked Scroggins.

"Can't fucking wait," the two men bumped fists with each other, slid open the side door of the van and jumped out.

CHAPTER 35

Gilday and Scroggins cautiously made their way up the sidewalk to McNeil's house. Armed policemen flanked them from the shadows surrounding the house. Gilday stepped up to the front door and pressed the buzzer. Scroggins stood to the side, weapon drawn. Gilday pressed the buzzer again and banged on the door with his fist.

"Bart? Hey Bart, it's Jeff Gilday! Open up, man!" Gilday banged on the door harder.

"He's not answering, boss," Scroggins whispered into his headset.

"Crack it. This is a Go signal, repeat, this is a Go signal."

Scroggins nodded to another policeman, who stepped forward with a battering ram. The officer smashed the front door in and Gilday and Scroggins bolted through it. Simultaneously, other officers broke through the back door and the bedroom windows.

"Police! Don't move!" Scroggins screamed.

Both men ran down the front hallway, which was cluttered with trash and old newspapers. Gilday and Scroggins fanned out, other officers following behind them. One group went down a hall into the kitchen, the other cut through the dining room. The noise of a television set could be heard from somewhere in the house.

"Bart? Bart, if you're here, speak up, man!" Gilday shouts.

"I got him! I got him!"

Scroggins stood at one end of the living room. A television, tuned to the Discovery Channel, played a program on lions. A man sat in front of the television in an easy chair with his back to Scroggins.

Scroggins aimed his weapon at the back of the man's head. Gilday appeared at the other side of the living room. The man didn't move and his arms sat comfortably on the armrests of the easy chair. The two men approached the chair cautiously.

"Bart! Bart, show me your hands!" Gilday yelled.

"PUT YOUR FUCKING HANDS UP, MCNEIL!" Scroggins screamed.

More officers joined Scroggins and Gilday in the living room, their weapons trained on McNeil. Everyone saw what was in McNeil's hand and it cranked the ass-pucker factor right up.

"Gun, he's got a gun!"

"Right hand!"

"Drop it! Drop it!"

"MCNEIL, I am going to FUCKING SHOOT you in the face if you don't drop the weapon and show me your hands RIGHT FUCKING NOW! MCNEIL!" Scroggins screamed.

Gilday and Scroggins took three slow steps and moved quickly around the front of McNeil on either side of the chair with weapons raised, ready to open fire.

They managed to hold their fire, but they didn't lower their weapons at their first sight of Bart McNeil. Gilday did, however, gag in spite of himself.

* * *

SOME TIME LATER, Thorne and Kane navigated their way through the cluttered front hallway of McNeil's house to the living room, where Forsythe and Hairston stood in front of the body of Bart McNeil. McNeil, a squat man in ratty boxer shorts and a T-shirt, sat comfortably in his easy chair, at least, as comfortable as a dead man could be. Scroggins and Gilday stood off to one side of the room, out of everyone's way, and stared at what was left of Bart McNeil.

The top of McNeil's head had been blown away and in his right hand he held an automatic pistol. Blood spatter covered the front of his shirt, but remarkably his face was untouched. A TV tray sat to one side of the chair, a bowl of dried stew and a half-empty bottle of Budweiser rested upon it. Forensic technicians scurried everywhere, taking pictures. Thorne and Kane kneeled down for a closer look at the body.

"Piece of shit saved us the cost of executing him," Forsythe said to them. "That's a forty-five in his hand. Stuck it in his mouth and blew the top of his head off. He must have figured that we were on to him."

"He was eating the children," Hairston said, still not quite believing it himself. "There's a pot of stew on the stove with fingers in it."

"Fucking sick fucking animal," Scroggins said. "I can't believe this."

"Captain, there are body parts in the refrigerator and in the freezer on the back porch," this from one of the other cops. "Fucking loads of parts."

"Nobody touch nothing, leave it for the techs."

"Did you see what was on top of the TV?" Hairston asked.

"What?" Kane stepped carefully over to the television. A

plastic baggie with some coarse dark hairs enclosed within it sat on top.

"Don't touch it," Forsythe barked. "I'll tell you what it is, it's hair, and I'll bet a year's salary it's pubic hair belonging to our DOA Boyd, this sneaky fucker got it and planted it."

"How convenient, left right out in the open for us," Thorne remarked. "How did an ice cream truck driver get the pubic hairs of a black man that lives fifty miles away?"

"Maybe he blew him in the back of some queer bar, who knows, who cares?"

"What about Darcy Mullens?" Kane asked.

One of the technicians, wearing rubber gloves, entered from the kitchen and held up a small pink snow jacket, a nametag sewn into the back collar.

"That's her jacket," Scroggins said, very grim. "Fuck me."

"What about her body?"

"Don't know. Won't know, until forensics can sort out the frozen food," the tech said.

"He's also got loads of trophies from other victims, shoes, clips of hair and jewelry," Gilday added. "Thorne?"

Thorne looked at him.

"Did you know he was eating them?"

Thorne didn't answer right away.

"You knew, didn't you, and you didn't say anything. You knew this guy was eating kids."

"He won't be eating any more of them," Thorne stood.

"It looks like we won't be needing either of you anymore," Forsythe said to Thorne and Kane. "We got our guy and we got a shitload of evidence to process. Why don't you do me a favor and get your ass clear of my crime scene?"

Thorne looked at Forsythe for a moment, expressionless, before turning to Kane.

"Let's go, Kane. This scene is dead."

"A fucking cannibal," Scroggins grimaced as Thorne walked by him. "Just like Jeffrey Dahmer, right, Thorne?"

"Except for one thing."

"What's that?"

"Dahmer didn't kill himself. Come on, Kane, shake a leg. Let's get some breakfast."

Thorne disappeared down the hallway. Kane stared for a moment at Darcy's pink snow jacket before following.

CHAPTER 36

Thorne exited the McNeil House and stood in the front yard, surveying the scene before him. Lights, cars and police personnel were everywhere, surrounding the house and covering the entire street.

Kane joined Thorne in the yard, zipping her jacket all the way up to her chin to protect herself from the bitterly cold wind, or so she told herself. She didn't remember being this cold before entering McNeil's but she definitely felt the chill now.

Bill Johnson, stitches still fresh on his forehead, borrowed a smoke from another officer out on the front lawn, both of them stamping their feet from the cold.

"Johnson!" Thorne barked, which caused the younger man to jump yet again. "Car keys!"

Johnson fumbled for the keys and tossed them to Thorne, who caught them easily. Johnson pointed at an unmarked sedan and Thorne walked slowly toward the car. Kane followed and then made a quick detour to some bushes in the neighbor's yard. She threw up. Thorne watched her as she retched.

"Come on, Kane, stop fucking around," he said after a moment. Thorne climbed into the sedan.

Kane wiped her mouth, embarrassed, and got into the passenger seat. Thorne put the keys into the ignition but did not start it. He pounded the steering wheel several times with his open hand.

"Something bothering you?"

"A lot of things bother me, Kane. You, for one."

"What is it?"

"Never mind," Thorne started the car, an angry glint in his eye.

"What is it?"

"Kane, shut your pie-hole."

"You didn't think he'd kill himself, did you?" Thorne didn't answer her. "You didn't profile him as a suicide, right?"

"No, I did not. And do you know why I did not profile him as a suicide?"

"Why?"

"Because he's not a fucking suicide, that's why," Thorne put the sedan into gear and spun out on the icy road, dodging police cars and news vans.

"He fits the profile, though, right? Except for that one thing, he's exactly what you said."

"Doesn't matter."

"Thorne, did you see what was inside that house?"

"Doesn't matter."

"If he's not the Iceman, how do you explain what we found in his fucking kitchen?"

"I'm not trying to explain it, I'm just telling you what I know. The Iceman is not a suicide. End of story."

"Maybe you're wrong on your profile."

"What have I told you about that?"

"Everybody is wrong once in awhile."

"Everybody but me."

Neither said another word to each other on the drive back to Lincoln.

CHAPTER 37

Kane walked down the hallway of cubicles at headquarters on her way to her desk to file yet another report. It seemed as though the three days since the discovery at Bart McNeil's house had just flown by in a media-drenched whirlwind of activity and her superiors were in the process of drowning her in paper and electronic reports.

Every aspect of the case was examined in minute detail again and again, not only by law enforcement agencies but also in the papers and on television across America. The air in the whole city, the state, maybe even the entire country, had lightened considerably. Laughter, actual laughter coming from people not inhabiting a sitcom, was heard in the hallways of offices and schools everywhere.

For certain, everyone mourned the children lost to the killer and felt for their families, but folks everywhere were almost weak with relief now that the ordeal was finally over. For a few days, Kevorkian and his Mercy Killings were put on the news back burner in favor of the events in Nebraska.

Kane kept her eye out for Thorne, whom she'd barely

seen the past three days. Thorne was around but somehow managed to disappear into the background. He came in, stared at his chessboard for awhile, ordered take-out and watched television before heading back to his room.

He wouldn't entertain any conversation about the case, or anything, for that matter. If asked a question, he would answer in as few words as possible, if at all. He left all the after-action reports for Kane to do on her own, something that still rankled her when she thought about it.

Thorne also avoided any media and managed to never be mentioned in print or on television. Kane had been through this before on the DC shooting and was a little more adept at dodging the press, though her picture still managed to find its way into the papers upon occasion.

Thorne just effortlessly sidestepped any and all attention, not that there was a lack of volunteers willing to step forward and speak in the national spotlight. Forsythe was at the head of that line and clearly enjoying his time in front of the cameras.

It was hard to even turn on a television without seeing Forsythe's meaty face going on about "the chase for the Iceman." There was gossip around the watercooler that he was already negotiating a book deal and was considering the possibility of retiring to pursue a career in radio. Rumor was that Forsythe had big plans to stretch his fifteen minutes into hours, days, weeks and hopefully years. Forsythe was one happy camper.

"Hey, Emma," Scroggins said, pouring himself coffee from a fresh pot in the break room. "Coffee?"

"Sure, black with lots of sugar," Kane joined him. She hadn't seen much of him or Gilday in the last three days either, though she caught glimpses of them in the hallway and occasionally on television in one of the many reports that played the Heartland Child Murders nonstop. "You've been pretty busy."

"You know, it's funny, while we were chasing this fuck, the captain kept Jeff and me outside the loop as much as he could. Now that we caught him, Captain Asshole doesn't want us out of his sight, wants us at every briefing, every meeting with Justice, you name it. He can't fart without us catching a whiff."

"He wants you to present a glowing report to your boss, so he's kissing your ass." Kane took a cup from him and blew on it, cooling the coffee.

"He can kiss my ass. We've been meaning to catch up with you and Thorne, Jeff and I both. We're going to make sure our boss knows what you guys did and how much help you were. Where is Thorne, anyway? I never see the grouchy bastard anymore."

"I was just going to look for him. He's not back at the motel, so he's hiding around here somewhere."

"I see they got you the latest update?" Scroggins nodded at the report in her hand.

"Yeah, just got it, Norman himself handed it to me. How are you doing?"

"I'm hanging in there, hell," Scroggins replied. "I'm just glad we got him. I would have preferred to shoot the son of a bitch myself, but I'll take what I can get."

"You look like you're feeling better."

"Yeah, it was a tough scene but yeah, I am better. I gotta tell you, I've been a trooper for ten years and a cop a lot longer than that, and I've seen some shit, like we all have. I've always managed to keep that, you know, wiseass cop distance from the job, you know how it is. This is the first time it ever got this personal, the fucking creep was practically in my backyard. That's my fucking home the prick was taking a shit in. These were people I knew and really cared about. It just … after finding McNeil's body and Darcy's coat, Jeff and I had to give the bad news to Chad and Barb and let me tell you, that was no picnic."

"I'm sorry, Gerry."

"Me too. Darcy was the best kid, I've known her all her life, she was really sweet and special and …" a dark cloud covered his face and Scroggins had to turn partially away for a moment. "It's just a fucking tragedy when it's someone you know real well. That's all. The funeral was last night, Jeff and I went and Barb and Chad lost it during the service, just lost it.

"But at least now they know for sure what happened and can try and move on," he continued. "They're young enough they could have more kids, if they want, I don't know. Important thing, it's all over. It's over for everyone and we can all move on. After I get all the paperwork and shit done, I'm going to have myself a nice stiff drink. Speaking of which …" he smiled at her, and she recognized the opening, got ready for it.

"Hey, what's going on over here?" Gilday joined them. "Did you guys see this?" he held up a newspaper, the headline of which read "ICEMAN ICES SELF!"

"I did see that one."

"Lord, we're gonna be reading shit like that for a long time," Scroggins said.

"How's it going, Emma?"

"Good, Jeff, how are you?"

"Better and better and it'll only go up from here. What are you two talking about?"

"Nothin', just shooting the shit," Scroggins replied.

"That's all?"

"Yes Jeff, that's all, Christ."

Thorne stalked by the break room without saying good morning to anyone and headed for his desk.

"I gotta talk to him, guys," Kane said, "I'll chat with you later." Kane started walking after Thorne.

"Hey, Emma, how much longer are you and Thorne sticking around?" Gilday asked.

"Not long at all, Captain Asshole wants us out of his hair and our boss wants us back ASAP," Kane replied over her shoulder. "I just got an email from our section chief. We're supposed to take the next flight out tonight."

"Oh, I don't think so," Scroggins said.

"Yeah, that's out of the question," Gilday chimed in.

"Why, what are you talking about?"

"There's a weather report on my desk, take a look at it when you go by."

"What, is it going to snow again?"

"You might say that."

"That's one way of putting it."

Kane raised her curious eyebrow at both of them and snatched the weather report off of Scroggins's desk as she walked by.

CHAPTER 38

Kane found Thorne at his usual spot in front of his chessboard, the Miles Davis song "So What" playing on his CD player. Thorne was on the phone and while he talked, Kane took a look at the weather report in her hand.

"Yeah, Pete, that's what they tell me," Thorne said into the phone. "Nothing's wrong, I am brimming with happiness and joy. I'm doing cartwheels down the street. I'm fucking high on life, Pete. Yeah. Yeah. Hey, whatever she wrote is fine by me. She handled the operation, a lippy broad but definitely functional for the most part, which is more than I can say for some people."

Kane noted the backhanded compliment Thorne had just paid to her as she finished the weather report. She sat down at her desk opposite Thorne.

"So enough of this happy horseshit, I hear we're flying back ASAP. So I'm back on Kevorkian? What's that? I didn't just hear what I heard, right? Pete. Pete? Do not fuck with me on this, all right? You gave me your word, doesn't that mean anything? Pete, I'm starting to not like you now. I don't care, just keep your fucking word," Thorne hung up on Viera and did so rather violently, in Kane's view.

Thorne hunched over his chessboard, selected a black bishop and captured a white knight. He spun the board around to consider the game from the other side.

"Are they going to let you work the Mercy Killings?" Kane asked.

"Eventually. Just not at the moment."

"That's bullshit, neither of these cases here would have been closed if it weren't for you. That's fucking bullshit."

"Yes, Kane. It is fucking bullshit. What do you want?"

"Couple things. Item one. The wealth of evidence recovered from McNeil's house over the last three days makes it now official. The Heartland Child Murders case is now considered closed and our perpetrator caught.

"The governor will be making a statement to that effect later on in the day. DNA and dental records confirmed that many of the body parts in the house belonged to several of the unaccounted for missing girls, at least one of whom has been missing for over a year. Found her remains in his freezer, along with some unidentified parts.

"They have officially linked seven names to him and his house so far and they expect that number to keep going up. Ballistics matched the forty-five in his hands to the bullets that were fired at us. The pubic hair in the baggie matched to Trent Boyd, we don't yet know how he got it but he somehow did.

"They even found Wendy Frederickson's pajamas. They haven't found the remains of Darcy Mullens as of yet, but they expect to. So it's official. Bart McNeil was the Iceman. We're done here," Kane looked at Thorne expectantly.

"If you say we're done, then I guess we must be done."

"Item two, I'm sure you got the email, they want us back

ASAP and to fly out tonight. Unfortunately, there's been an added wrinkle."

"What?"

"I just got the weather report from Gerry. Major winter storm heading our way, going to hit here in two or three hours."

"So?"

"So no flights out, they're canceling everything, telling people not to even drive. We're talking one mother of a blizzard, two feet of snow and eighty mile an hour winds. We can't fly out for at least a day, maybe longer. We're stuck here."

"Great. We've won the Lotto. First prize, a trip to Nebraska. Second prize, two trips to Nebraska. Fucking Pete," Thorne moved a white rook and reversed the board again to play black.

"Thorne?"

"What?"

"What's the real reason you play chess against yourself?"

"That's one of those questions that, if you have to ask it, then you won't understand the answer."

Scroggins and Gilday joined Kane and Thorne. Scroggins held out his hand to Thorne.

"Agent Thorne, I just wanted to say that it was a real pleasure watching you work."

"Yeah, me too," Gilday also held out his hand. "None of this would have been possible if it weren't for you and we would have never gotten to the end of this thing."

Thorne sighed, leaned forward and with both hands grasped each man by the right wrist and quickly joined them together, making them shake hands with each other and thus avoiding the exercise himself.

"Thank each other."

The two large men laughed as they shook hands. Thorne reclined back in his chair.

"You're a crazy bastard, Thorne, but I like ya," Gilday said.

Scroggins quickly swiveled to Kane.

"Emma, it's been great working with you, too."

"Yeah, Emma, it's been a real pleasure, and I was wondering if you would be interested …"

"If you would like to go out to dinner with me," Scroggins interrupted Gilday.

"Hey, I started first!" Gilday protested.

"And I finished first!"

"You sneaky son of a bitch …"

"Hey, whoa, fellas, what the hell?" Kane waved her hands. "What's going on?"

"Would you go out to dinner with me?" Gilday asked.

"Or would you go out to dinner with me?"

"Go out with one of us, at least."

"Who said I'm going to go out with anybody?"

"You're single, you're free. You have to go out with somebody, why not one of us?"

"You can't argue with that logic, Hotlips," Thorne said.

"I don't HAVE to go out with anybody."

"Hell, Emma, after all we've been through," Scroggins said, "the least you could do is to go to dinner with one of us."

"Besides, you're snowed in, so why not?" Gilday added.

"Why don't the three of us have dinner together?"

"Hah! Knew she was a kinky one," Thorne snorted.

"Gerry and I couldn't do that, it would ruin our fun but competitive friendship."

"He's right, there would be a weird vibe. You'll just have to choose one of us," Scroggins said.

"I can't just choose between you two guys, and besides, the most I will agree to is just a friendly dinner."

"That's cool with us, we're friendly guys. Pick one of us for a friendly dinner."

"Pick one. We'll be fine either way, whoever you pick. Honest. Which will it be?"

Kane looked at Thorne, who shrugged.

"Don't look at me," he replied, "if it weren't for the nametags I wouldn't even be able to tell them apart."

"Come on, Emma, we're nice guys, give one of us country boys a break."

"Well," Kane was charmed despite herself. "All right. Dinner. Just dinner."

"Great. Who's it going to be?"

"Who's it going to be?"

"Do I have to pick just one of you?"

"Yes, absolutely."

"Absolutely, no other way around it."

"Well then. I'm going to have to say ... Gerry."

"Yes!"

"But only because he asked me first, really, Jeff."

"I started to ask first, but butthead here interrupted me."

"Gerry started to ask me in the break room and I never answered, really that's the only reason," Kane said.

"Really?"

"I hinted at it, buddy, I didn't really come out and straight out ask her, honest."

"Cheater."

"If we're stuck here another day then I'll have dinner with you tomorrow night, my word on that Jeff," Kane said.

"I will go out and do my snow dance then, just so you'll have to stay," Gilday replied. "Gerry, you cheating bastard."

"All right!" Scroggins rubbed his hands together.

"But listen, Gerry," Kane said, "it's just dinner, it's not a real date, okay?"

"Hey, I'll take whatever I can get. Pick you up here at six?"

"Sure."

Scroggins walked away happily, pumping his fist in the air. "Yes! Yeah boy, yeah!"

"If that's how excited he gets for a dinner between friends," Thorne observed, "then I don't want to be in the room when he gets a real date."

"Word of warning," Gilday said. "When he puts Bon Jovi on the stereo, that's when he's gonna make his move."

"Thanks, Jeff, but there will be no moves, trust me," she replied. "It's not a real date, it's just dinner, really."

"Okay, just remember, Bon Jovi, the slow power ballad, that's when he's going for it," Gilday pointed a finger gun salute at them both, fired and then walked away.

Kane felt the weight of Thorne's gaze and looked at him.

"It's not a real date," she said. "It's not."

CHAPTER 39

The blizzard hit at six-thirty and hit hard. Sheets of snow swirled in thick clouds over the highways and visibility was next to nothing. Snowplows worked nonstop but as soon as they removed snow, more piled on. A traveler's advisory was changed to a traveler's warning, which in turn became a blanket announcement on all stations warning everyone to stay off the roads and to stay home.

Thorne sat in his usual spot at headquarters, feet up on the table with a view of both his chessboard and the map of Nebraska on the wall. Charlie "Bird" Parker played on his CD player, digging into his classic "K.C. Blues." Next to Nina Simone, Charlie Parker was probably Thorne's favorite jazz stylist, but the usual comfort that came from the Bird at work was slow to arrive this night and that frustrated Thorne almost as much as the chess game.

It was a touchy spot in the game and there were few pieces left on his chessboard for either side. Thorne considered the game from the white point of view. Hairston and Johnson walked by busily and stopped when they saw him.

"Agent Thorne?" Hairston asked. "What are you still doing here?"

"Nothing good on cable."

"I'm assuming your flight was delayed or cancelled?"

"Assume away, Norman."

"Oh. Well, we're on a skeleton crew tonight, but Sergeant Johnson and I will be here for awhile catching up on some paperwork, so if you need anything…"

"If I need anything, Norman, I will scream and I will shout."

Hairston and Johnson glanced at each other. Thorne was one strange bird, as had been discussed around the office more than once, and one had to wonder how in the hell someone like him got a badge and a gun.

He was possibly a dangerous bird as well. There was scuttlebutt that Thorne and the captain had perhaps had a small altercation in the toilet, one the captain was on the losing end of, which was hard to believe since Forsythe was six inches taller and a hundred pounds heavier. Forsythe steadfastly denied any such altercation occurred and denied it rather hotly as well. The captain maintained that he slipped and fell on the wet floor and while he was on the floor, Thorne asked him to recommend a good restaurant.

Either story was unsettling and strange. One thing was certain, the captain may hate Thorne no less than he did before, but he sure as hell was less open about it than previously. All of which added fuel to the rumor fire that Thorne was not a person to be trifled with.

Not that Johnson would even think of trifling with him, from day one Thorne scared the bejesus out of him. Hairston and Johnson shrugged and left Thorne to hunch over his chessboard while in the care of Charlie "Bird" Parker.

CHAPTER 40

Kane, a bottle of wine in hand, followed Scroggins into his house. Kane hadn't been on a date in quite some time. Actually, it'd been years since her last one. Much of her personal life had gotten put into cold storage since The Van Incident. Since getting out of the force and accepted into Quantico, she hadn't thought that it would ever be any other way, but here she was. Kane took off her coat and hung it on the rack. They both kicked off their snow boots, cheeks ruddy from the cold.

"Welcome to the house of Gerry!" Scroggins opened his arms.

Scroggins's house was well kept and clean, Kane noted, a dining room with a table already set for dinner, a snug living room complete with a fire already burning in the fireplace and a flight of stairs that led up to the second floor, leading, Kane assumed, to his bedroom. It is probably better if the particulars of that room are left solely to my imagination, Kane thought to herself. A very cozy house, not quite what Kane imagined a single guy like Scroggins would have all by his lonesome.

"This is a beautiful home. My God. Something smells really good."

"I told you, I can cook, seriously cook real food that folks can actually eat. Just a second," Scroggins reached past Kane to punch in a code into the alarm box next to the front door. His face came within inches of hers and she caught a whiff of cologne, which she found quite pleasing, very conscious of him at that moment.

"Sorry, I always have the alarm on. I guess being a cop has made me ultra security conscious."

"Me too."

Kane, in her stocking feet, followed Scroggins into his kitchen and set the wine on the counter. She was struck by a feeling of comfort and safety. It reminded her of her childhood, sitting in a cozy kitchen filled with warmth and wonderful smells while the wind pounded on the windows outside.

It took her by surprise, this feeling, she hadn't thought about her childhood or anything to do with growing up in a long time. Being a child and being a cop were often points of view diametrically opposed. That Scroggins was able to resurrect that memory, even unintentionally, caused Kane to smile wide at him, in spite of herself.

"So what's for dinner?"

"You're gonna love it, I dug this recipe up … wait a minute, shit. You're not a vegetarian, are you?"

"Not yet. But I have been considering it."

CHAPTER 41

A couple of hours later and Thorne was still in front of his chessboard. He listened to his other favorite, Nina Simone, on the CD player. She crooned her classic "I Put A Spell On You" at high volume. Thorne had been alternating Nina and Charlie, hoping for relief.

The wind howled against the windows but Thorne was oblivious, concentrating only on his game while deep within the rhythm of the song.

He'd always been capable of this. He had the ability to lose himself within a game and solid jazz. His concentration was so focused that much of the outside world at that point ceased to exist. Thorne put himself in this place in his mind and usually, at some point, the answer he sought would come. Thorne was a big believer in observable fact and old school math, but by themselves they weren't strong enough to find an answer, they needed inspiration and imagination in order to be complete. Almost always they came together before the end of a game. Almost always.

Thorne carefully moved his black knight forward, now within striking distance of the white king. The trap was set.

CHAPTER 42

After dinner had been served, eaten and the dishes loaded and humming away in the dishwasher, Kane and Scroggins settled on the couch in front of the fireplace to finish off the bottle of red wine that Kane had brought.

Kane was red-faced and giggling, feeling the intoxicating effect of both the wine and the attractive company she was keeping.

"You think that's funny, this one is even better," Scroggins said. "This guy's parked out on the highway, taking a major piss right out in front of God and everybody, blitzed out of his skull and I get there, jump out, weapon drawn, being the eager young rookie that I was, and I shout 'Hold it! Put your hands in the air!' And he turned toward me, dick in his hand, and says, 'Well which is it? You want my hands in the air or you want me to hold it? I can't do BOTH!'"

Kane went from giggling to outright laughter. Scroggins poured her more wine, finishing off the bottle.

"Okay, Kane, there's something I just gotta know."

"What's that, Scroggins?"

"Here's the thing that I do not understand. Now, you may not be aware of this, but you're a very attractive woman."

"Am I?"

"Absolutely. Not that something like that is important to me, not at all."

"I'm sure it's not."

"Right. But what I do not understand is how a woman as attractive as you could possibly be single, available and sitting next to me on my couch. It's beyond my comprehension as a male."

"Well, I am well armed, so that might have something to do with it."

"That's not something that I consider a drawback; in fact, it only adds to your allure. Seriously, though, there's never been anyone you thought about, you know, settling with?"

"There was someone in DC, another cop. We lived together for awhile, but things happened. It ended about a year or so ago."

"What happened?"

Kane blinked and recalled everything in an instant. The turmoil of the events in the van took an immediate toll on her love life. She just completely lost all interest in Tim, both physically and emotionally, after The Van Incident. They saw a counselor together and she of course saw the department shrink, but it was over and done the moment she climbed out of that river.

In fact, she never thought about him at all anymore, unless a picture or a specific question brought her back to that time. Five years with Tim and all of a sudden it was as if they never happened. It must have hurt him terribly when she left.

"It would be fair to say that the job got in the way of the relationship."

"It does that, doesn't it?"

"What about you?" Kane asked him. "How is it that an attractive man such as yourself with his own house and excellent culinary skills is still single and available?"

"You know, I was just wondering about that myself."

"Were you?"

"Oh yeah, hell, I think I'm a good catch. I just haven't been caught yet. I think it's just a matter of timing. It hasn't yet been time, but hopefully that time will be soon."

"What about Barb Mullens?"

"Oh shit, you talked to Jeff, he's trying to cock-block me. Look. Barb and me? Ancient history. Really. I mean, you never forget your first crush, right? Answer this. Who was your first big time love?"

"Darin Hartzler, eighth grade."

"That's what I'm saying, you don't forget your first. That was Barb and me, we were the homecoming couple at high school, the whole deal. But when I enlisted and went away, she fell in love with Chad Mullens. Shit happens. I like Chad, he's a good man. Thing is, like, after I got my badge and moved back home, back to town, I used to hang out with the both of them, we went to dinner together, bowling, we were friends. Bunch of us that went to school together hung out, Jeff and me and … well, nobody else you would know, but a bunch of us. We all socialized.

"The problem was when I started working night shift and Chad and everyone else worked days. That's when it started to get hinky, not for us but for everybody else. I was off during the day and since Barb is a housewife and home at the same time, we'd do things, run errands, take Darcy out for a ride, all that. Sometimes folks in town would see Barb and me having lunch or walking in the park in the afternoon and they would, you know, they would talk."

"They thought you two had hooked back up again."

"Yeah, small towns, that's how it is. Someone thought

something and then someone else started talking, even though nothing happened, everybody talked like it did. And even though it was all talk and bullshit, it caused tension, to the point Chad started saying things. So a couple of years ago, Barb and Chad and me just sort of stopped being social at all.

"It hurt, because I liked them, we'd all been friends forever, and I loved Darcy, she was a real sweetheart. It was a tough thing but it was for the best, it really was. Small town gossip can get nasty and not only could it have hurt their marriage, it could have cost me my job. A trooper can get IAD'd right out of a job for adultery. They take that shit seriously in Nebraska. Even a hint of impropriety can hurt you. That's why I'm a bit touchy about it. My job is everything to me, you know what I'm saying?"

That question caused Kane to start thinking again, remembering how pleased she was the day she got her badge, how Tim had wanted her to quit after The Van Incident and how angry that had made her.

"Yeah. I do."

"So tell me, Emma," Scroggins leaned forward so that his face was only a few inches away from hers.

"Tell you what?"

"Why'd you decide to work in law enforcement?"

"I like guns."

"Me too. They don't let you use them, most other jobs."

"I know! Can you believe that?"

Scroggins leaned a little closer to her face. Kane evaded him by taking a strategic sip of wine. Scroggins smiled good-naturedly, leaned back and stretched. He picked up the remote control to the stereo and turned it on.

The song, "Always," by Bon Jovi, began to play softly at low volume. Kane sighed and set her jaw. This would be a hell've a lot easier if she didn't actually like him so much.

Damn it all, who would've thought, in Nebraska of all places?

A howling wind shook the windows.

"Listen to that wind," Scroggins said.

"Gerry."

"It's nasty out there. You know what?"

"What?"

"You just might have to spend the night."

"Gerry."

"What? We get snowed in, we get snowed in."

"Gerry."

"I don't have any control over the weather, that's out of my hands, what am I supposed to do?"

"Gerry."

"What?"

"You're a great guy, but ..."

"Thank you."

"But ..."

"But what?"

"But THIS is just a friendly dinner. This ... is NOT ... a DATE."

"It's friendly, I'm friendly and you're friendly," Scroggins leaned in close to Kane again.

"It's friendly but it is not a date."

This time Kane let his face get close to hers.

"A friendly non-date dinner between two attractive ..."

"Not a date."

"Two attractive and available people not on a date. That's what's happening here. That's all, nothing else," Their faces were close enough now that their lips nearly touched.

"Nothing else."

Scroggins kissed Kane and was caught off guard by the passion with which she returned his kiss. Kane grabbed the hair on the back of his head and kissed him with a hunger that surprised even her, a hunger she thought she wouldn't be feeling ever again.

Kane ripped open Scroggins's flannel shirt and took it off of him as she kissed him again and again, running her hands over his chest, catching her fingers in the hair there, something she always liked doing to men.

Scroggins pulled her shirt out of her slacks, lost his balance on the couch and then the two of them toppled off and onto the floor. They laughed and kissed again, taking more time with it but with no less passion or excitement. They kissed and then some.

CHAPTER 43

Charlie "Bird" Parker wailed away at his classic "Now's The Time," Thorne's personal favorite composition from the Bird. In fact, when the song ended, Thorne skipped back and played it again, so far five times in a row, waiting for the "Bird" to bring him home.

Thorne moved the white queen to block the dark knight that threatened the white king. He turned the board around to consider it from the black side. Thorne made another move and put the dark rook in position. He spun the board and examined the white position. Other than to move chess pieces, Thorne had not stirred from his desk for hours.

"Agent Thorne?"

Thorne glanced up to see Johnson staring at him.

"What?"

"It's one o'clock in the morning."

"So?"

Thorne moved his white queen again, countering the black attack. He spun the board back around.

"So, uh," Johnson stuttered, "Norm's been gone for awhile and ... I think I'm gonna go home now."

"So go."

Johnson blinked. He turned and went back to his desk. Norm had said to stick around as long as the fibbie did and it sure didn't look like he was going to able leave any time soon.

Thorne made his final move with a dark knight. He leaned back.

Checkmate.

Fucking checkmate.

Black wins.

It's over.

"FUCK!"

Thorne angrily swept the chessboard off of the table. He stood and kicked a desk chair across the room. Johnson, startled by the sudden noise, ran over from his desk and stopped a few feet away from the FBI agent, struck dumb by the sight of Thorne in a rage.

"MOTHERFUCKER! COCKSUCKER!" Thorne pounded the table with his fist. He noticed Johnson.

"You know what REALLY bothers me about this whole fucking thing?" Thorne said. "Besides everything? Look at this, fucking look at this," Thorne pointed at the map of Nebraska.

"The first kill was WAY over here, in North Platte, hundreds of miles away from where McNeil lives. What's the first rule, what's the first thing they hammer into your skull at the academy?"

"What?"

"First rule in school, serial killers start close to home and work out. That's how it is, ninety-five percent of the time. But not our Iceman, he's onto us, knows the rules already, seen the movies, knows every contact leaves a trace, knows to leave false forensics, knows basically what we look for and for some reason went backwards to end up ten miles away from where he lived."

"But …"

"Question one. You think McNeil was that smart? Answer, no, he was not. Question two. Where was he really going? What was he working towards? Was his goal to kill little girls until he got to his neighborhood and then take his own life? And if so, why?"

"Well, he must have known that we were onto him."

"How? How could he fucking know what we were doing? Look at the Iceman's pattern. A straight, very nearly evidence-free line to Denton, Nebraska. We get to Denton and a fingerprint is LITERALLY dropped at our doorstep. A fingerprint that leads to a suspect that ALMOST fits the profile, a suspect who is very conveniently dead as Dillinger AND has a house full of evidence. Question three. Is every number and decimal point in this equation accounted for? Answer. No. It doesn't fucking add up."

"But we got him, right?"

"You … NOT listening. McNeil … NOT smart enough. Why are you still here? Go home. Get the fuck out of here!"

Johnson walked quickly back to his desk, anxious to get away from Thorne, reflexively grabbing recently arrived faxes from the fax machine. Thorne was definitely a grumpy scary fucker and Johnson just knew he was going to be stuck here all night with this cuckoo.

Thorne kicked his desk. He stalked over to the map of Nebraska and glared at it. Charlie "Bird" Parker worked on his temper and Thorne finally relaxed and sighed. Thorne noticed a computer printer next to one of the desks.

It was an Epson Stylus 700.

"I am a fucking simpleton," Thorne said to himself. "Johnson!"

Johnson popped back up like a prairie dog, too scared to disobey.

"Who uses this printer?"

"Everybody on this side of the room, Agent Kane, Gerry, Jeff, you. Andy. Me. Why?" Johnson blew a sigh, wondering when this night would be over and he would be quit of this whacko fed. He flipped through the faxes in his hand.

"Why?" Thorne grabbed his jacket. "We're a long way past why! I need a car and I need it now, Johnson!"

Johnson, suddenly startled by one of the faxes in his hand, froze before he could answer.

"Johnson! You're not listening again! What is it?"

"This came in an hour ago and it's probably a joke, but …"

Eyes narrowing, Thorne swiped the paper from Johnson. He read it and looked up at Johnson.

"Can you find whose number this is?"

"Yeah, I just have to …"

"Do it!"

Johnson scurried off.

Thorne looked at the fax again. Scrawled in large block letters, it read:

TO: THORNE

FR: ICEMAN

RE: THE HEARTLAND CHILD MURDERS

DEAR FEDERAL JAGOFF,

TASTE NEEDS TO BE TAUGHT.

Thorne dug into his pocket for his cell phone.

"Shit," Thorne said. "Kane."

CHAPTER 44

The noise of the storm woke Kane.

She was wrapped in Scroggins's arms in his bed, naked and warm under several quilts and a thick comforter. Kane did get to see his bedroom after all and it was everything she thought it would be. Kane glanced at the alarm clock on the table next to the bed. Half past one and the blizzard was still going strong.

Kane looked at Scroggins asleep next to her. He snored and though it was a bit loud, it was kind of cute, too. She gently moved his arms off of her and slid out of bed. Scroggins snorted and rolled over on his side away from her. He wrapped the comforter around him and snored even louder.

This noise might be a problem in the future, if we have one. Don't want to think about that now, Kane thought. Great sex, great release and that's good enough. For now.

Kane sat on the bed and fished for her panties under the covers. In the movies people always seemed wake up after a marathon sex session still clad, magically, in their underwear. Kane had to look for hers and in the dark, too.

Her panties were the only article of clothing to make the trip upstairs to the bedroom, everything else got left downstairs on the couch when Gerry scooped her up in his arms and carried her to bed. She finally found her panties and slid them on. Putting on one of his T-shirts, Kane padded out of the bedroom.

There's another bathroom up here, if she remembered correctly, right down the hall from the bedroom. Kane found it and sat on the toilet without turning on the light. Kane peed and giggled at herself. I'm already comfortable enough here that I use the bathroom with the door open, she thought.

Kane flushed the toilet and stepped out of the bathroom. She heard a strange noise downstairs and stopped before going back to the bedroom. She tiptoed to the stairs and peeked down to the lower landing.

Nothing seemed out of the ordinary. The fire in the fireplace had burned itself down to glowing embers. Kane heard it again, the noise, a low buzzing noise. Her weapon lay on the coffee table where she'd left it. She tiptoed downstairs to the living room.

The buzzing noise got louder. Kane picked up her pistol and searched for the source. The light on the alarm panel next to the front door was still green. Okay, she thought, that means nobody has come in or gone out.

So where was that noise coming from?

Kane tracked the buzzing sound and found that it was coming from her pants on the floor. She picked her pants up and took her cell phone out of the pocket. She'd left it on vibrate but it ceased buzzing before she could answer. Went to voicemail. The phone screen informed her that she had missed several calls. She didn't recognize any of the numbers but it was probably Thorne, fucking with her. Fuck him, she was off duty.

Kane sighed and set the phone and gun aside for a moment in order to put her pants back on. She picked them back up and headed back to bed, phone in one hand and gun in the other.

Her cell phone vibrated again on her way up the stairs, startling her.

"Hello?" she answered.

"Kane, where the fuck are you?"

"Thorne?" Kane whispered. "Why are you calling me, don't you ever sleep?"

"Where the fuck are you?"

"What do you care, where the fuck are you?" Kane retorted.

Some miles away, Johnson navigated his truck with great care through a wall of swirling snow on the highway while Thorne talked to Kane on his cell phone from the passenger seat. Johnson was pale and shivering and not just from the bitter cold. He was very scared, he'd lived in Nebraska all his life and he knew that people who got stuck outside in weather like this often froze to death.

"Goddamn it," Thorne said. "Where are you, are you shacked up with Scroggins at his house?"

"That information is none of your goddamn business."

"Listen to me and answer the fucking question, Kane! Are you with Scroggins?"

"You're going mental, Thorne. Yes, I am with Gerry at his house," Kane whispered into her phone. "We're both adults and fuck you if you don't like it. I'm hanging up and turning off my phone now."

Kane slid back into the bedroom. Scroggins was still rolled over on his side and snoring. Kane set her weapon on the table next to the bed.

"Wait, Kane! We tried calling his home but the phone line

at his house is out. Is he there? Have you been with him all night?"

"Yes, all right?" Kane whispered. "I'm looking at him right now. Why?"

"Where was he at eleven-thirty?"

"In bed, Thorne. We were both in bed. Why?"

Kane slipped into bed and poked Scroggins, who was still snoring, with her free hand. He grunted but didn't wake up.

"The Iceman is still alive," Thorne said over the phone.

"What?"

"The Iceman is still alive, MacNeil isn't the Iceman. The Iceman sent me a fax at eleven-thirty. The number I got the fax from is Scroggins's home number, you understand me? I got a letter from the Iceman and it was faxed FROM Gerry Scroggins's house!"

"It's not Gerry, can't be …"

"It's either him or somebody else is in the house," Thorne's phone crackled with static interference.

Kane noticed the closet door opposite the bed was cracked open just a tiny bit. It hadn't been open before, that she knew. It had been closed tightly. She'd been looking at it while on top of Gerry. It had definitely been closed. She nudged Scroggins again.

"Gerry," Kane whispered. "Wake up."

"We can't get hold of the local PD out there, everything's fucked because of the blizzard. We're on the way to you now but we gotta wade through the snow!"

The closet door slowly creaked open an inch wider and stopped. Kane's eyes widened. She grabbed her weapon off the nightstand and pointed it at the closet.

"Kane, you'd better get out of that house!"

"He's here," Kane whispered into her cell phone. "I think he's here in the room."

"Don't try and take him, Kane, just get out of the house!"

The closet door creaked open a bit more. Kane set the phone down on the nightstand but left the phone open and connected to Thorne's call. The end of Kane's pistol shook. She poked Scroggins with her free hand.

"Gerry? Gerry, wake up."

The closet door creaked open another inch. Kane brought her free hand back to her grip on the pistol and tried desperately to steady her aim. The closet door creaked open an inch more and then in a rush it fell all the way open.

The dead body of Gerry Scroggins fell out of the bedroom closet and onto the floor, throat cut and eyes staring wide.

The man in the bed next to Kane suddenly leapt up on top of Kane as she screamed in terror. The Iceman punched Kane in the face and knocked the weapon out of her hand. Kane's pistol flew across the room and discharged, leaving a bullet in the ceiling of the bedroom and the smell of cordite in the air.

The Iceman got a hand around her throat and another one around both of her wrists. Kane slid one of her legs out from under him, wedged her foot against his waist and gave a big push. It wasn't enough to get him completely off but created just enough distance for Kane to free one of her hands.

"Kane!" Thorne screamed from the cell phone. "Get out of there!"

Kane punched the Iceman in the face and knocked him off the bed. Kane dove off of the other side of the bed and searched frantically for her weapon.

It lay on the other side of the room and she scrambled on all fours for it. Just as she put her hand on her weapon, the Iceman kicked it away.

The Iceman zapped Kane on the side of her neck with an electronic stun gun and knocked her out. He rolled her over onto her back, checked her pulse and opened one of her eyes to take a look at the dilated pupil.

"Such lovely eyes," he said.

"Kane?" Thorne shouted over the cell phone. "KANE!"

The Iceman picked up the cell phone from the nightstand and delicately hung it up.

CHAPTER 45

"You fucker!" Thorne screamed into the phone. "I'm fucking coming for you, you hear me?"

Johnson gripped the wheel even tighter as the truck slid on the snow and ice on the highway.

"Fuck me! Motherfucker!" Thorne slammed his phone into the dash, breaking it.

Johnson began to lose control of the truck. "I can't see where I'm … shit!"

The truck hit a large drift piled up on the highway and then spun into the ditch until they came to a stop with an explosion of snow. Johnson gunned it, the tires spinning, but the truck didn't move.

"Goddamn it! Punch it!" Thorne yelled.

"We're stuck, the snow's too heavy, we'll have to wait for a plow. You didn't break your phone, did you? How are we gonna call for …"

"What's that light over there?" Thorne pointed out into the darkness and blowing snow where a light could just barely be seen.

"I think it's a farmhouse or something," Johnson replied.

Thorne gave Johnson one of his looks.

"What?" Johnson asked.

CHAPTER 46

"Don't you fucking say a word!"

An elderly farmer and his wife, both clad in pajamas and bathrobes, stood in their kitchen and watched as Thorne screamed into their telephone.

Johnson stood shivering, microphone in hand, next to the farmer's Citizen Band radio. Both Johnson and Thorne were completely covered in snow.

"Forsythe, I don't want to hear any of your mealy mouthed SHIT, I don't care WHO you have to wake up, I want you to … Forsythe? Forsythe? Motherfucker HUNG UP ON ME! MOTHERFUCKER!"

Thorne threw the telephone furiously across the room into a wall.

"Told you he didn't want to talk to you. I finally got hold of Denton PD on the CB," Johnson said. "Couple of part-time cops. Gerry lives only a couple miles outside of town, they're gonna swing by as soon as they can."

"Would anyone like coffee?" the farmer's wife asked.

"They won't BE there anymore! FUCK!"

"It's no problem, if you want some coffee," she opened the freezer and took out a can of Folgers.

"I'd love some coffee," Johnson said.

"No, you don't want any fucking coffee, Johnson, we're moving out of here right now," Thorne said.

"To where? Where are we going? If they're not at Gerry's house, then where are they?"

"Only one place it could be but we have very little time. How far are we from town now?" Thorne asked the farmer.

"A good five, six miles."

"Can we borrow your truck? It's an emergency."

"We won't make it, not even with a truck. We had a truck," Johnson objected, although he did so carefully, mindful of the evil look in Thorne's eye. "The plows aren't even getting through, we got hit with three feet of snow and it's still coming down."

"Then we'll WALK it, Johnson!"

"You don't hafta walk," the farmer said.

"I'm not going to just sit ... what was that?"

"I said you don't hafta walk, if it's an emergency like you said it was."

Thorne looked at the farmer, who in turn looked at Johnson.

Johnson sighed.

CHAPTER 47

Moments later, in the blinding wind and snow, Thorne drove a large snowmobile wildly through the dark white night, hopefully in the direction of town. Johnson hung on for dear life behind him and wondered what he'd done to deserve such punishment as he was getting at this very moment.

CHAPTER 48

Kane opened her eyes and blinked a few times to orient herself. She tried to speak and realized that it was not possible. Her mouth was covered with duct tape. Kane tried to move and realized that she couldn't do that either.

She was handcuffed firmly to a metal chair, facing a big metal cooking table.

Looking around, she recognized where she was, having been all over this place just a few days earlier. She was at Denton Elementary School, in the kitchen of the school cafeteria, to be exact.

Darcy Mullens sat on the other side of the table opposite of Kane; the young girl's mouth also taped shut and hands taped to a chair. Darcy's eyes were wide open with fright and filled with tears.

The Iceman entered the kitchen, whistling.

He set a cloth-covered tray on the table between them. He wore surgical gloves on his hands. He stepped to the counter behind them, picked up a mini-grill and lugged it over to the table, setting it on top of it. He plugged it in so it could warm up.

The Iceman unloaded some groceries from a box, setting down green onions, cabbage, flour and eggs next to bowls and plates on the table.

He took the cloth off of the tray with a flourish, revealing knives of different shapes and sizes. The Iceman sat down next to Darcy, who whimpered in fear. He reached across the table and in one smooth motion ripped the tape from Kane's mouth.

Kane gasped, letting out a breath.

"Why didn't you want to have dinner with me, Emma?" Jeff Gilday asked.

CHAPTER 49

"I mean, Gerry's a good guy, but dumb as a rock," Gilday calmly started chopping up onions. "How could you pick him instead of me for dinner?"

"In retrospect," Kane answered, "I can't help but think that I made the best possible choice."

"Barb Mullens did the same thing in high school, chose Gerry over me. Never understood it."

"Maybe she was allergic to killers."

"I never killed anybody when I was in high school, although I probably should have. Besides, she hooked up with Gerry again a few years ago and he killed people in the war."

"They didn't hook up again, Gerry told me about that. Nothing happened."

"Yeah, I was listening and I couldn't believe you bought that bullshit story. They definitely had an affair years ago. I know because I followed them. Chad caught on and they almost divorced. Him and Barb ended up staying together for this little snot-nosed kid here. Didn't socialize with Gerry anymore, that's for damn sure.

"Gerry liked to spin it as a rumor thing, he played that card really well, but I know better. They were definitely making the beast with two backs. I staked them out. I took pictures. I dropped the note to Chad. I just could not believe it. She picked Gerry over me not once but twice. I was really pissed off."

"So you decided to vent a little anger by killing children?" Kane asked.

"Actually, I primarily wanted this one here," he gestured to Darcy. "Teach Barb and Gerry a lesson, you know. I couldn't really start with her, however, too dangerous, so I decided to start west and work my way here. That way by the time I got to her she would be just one victim out of many.

"I will admit it was a lot more fun than I thought it could be. I had a lot of really great meals in this very kitchen. But Darcy was the one I originally wanted. She has lovely blue eyes, don't you think? Just like Barb. You know who else has blue eyes like that?"

"Who?" Kane asked.

"Come on, you know who. Who were you playing naked twister with a few hours ago?"

"You think Gerry …"

"I'm not saying anything, I'm just saying. Different shades of blue, though, and that should be considered. That's what I think. Gerry sure did get worked up when I took her though, didn't he? Laughed my ass off, this fucking guy, always acted like his shit didn't stink. All bullshit and Barb never saw through it."

"I thought Gerry was your friend!"

"Gerry was varsity; he thought everyone was his friend. He was varsity and I was always second string, since we were twelve. That's what's so ironic. Tonight was supposed to be a quiet dinner just between Barb and myself, that was the original idea," Gilday moved on from the onions to the cabbage, chopping with quick deliberate strokes. "Barb Mullens was supposed to be sitting where you are right now.

"But I just couldn't believe you picked Gerry over me as well. I couldn't fucking believe it. As mad as I had been at Barb, I was even more pissed off at you. You didn't know me as a pimply fucking teenager, you have no excuse in picking Gerry over me. None," Gilday paused, eyes now hot with anger. "So tonight I cook for you."

"You planted everything on McNeil," Kane stalled, trying to think of something, anything.

"It was easy, too. I forced him to touch her eye. I thought Thorne would never get the eye clue, for Christ's sake, I practically had to spell it out for him. Some expert. I also made McNeil share some dinner with me, just in case you checked his stomach contents. He bawled like a baby, but he finished his meal. Put a gun to a person's head, it's amazing what they can make themselves do, don't you think?"

"I don't know, let me have my gun back and I'll find out."

"Oh, you'll be finding out, don't worry."

Gilday finished chopping the cabbage. He cracked eggs into a bowl and whisked. Darcy Mullens whimpered again, mucous running down from her nose.

"For dinner tonight we'll be starting with seasoned hot blood soup. It comes out hot, did you know that?"

"How can you do this, Jeff, how can you eat children?"

"They taste good. It's not that different from eating veal, really. If fact, it tastes better," Gilday finished with the eggs and poured some olive oil on the grill. It sizzled.

"For the entrée, we'll be having a dish called *Okonomiyaki*. Japanese, have you heard of it? It's delicious, a big favorite in Osaka. The best way to describe it would be as a grilled meat and egg pancake with special seasoning. In Japan they use seafood or beef, but of course I have a more flavorful substitute in mind for us."

"When did it happen, Jeff?"

"When did what happen, Emma?"

"When did the theme music from Looney Tunes start playing nonstop in your head, twenty-four-seven?"

"I'm not crazy, Emma."

"You're EATING KIDS, Jeff, you crossed the line of sanity a long time ago. You are a fruitcake psycho-killer!"

Gilday laughed gently. "We're all killers. You think Gerry was a better man than me, is that why you fucked him on the first date? He killed people in Iraq. We both did, even after the war was over. Especially after it was over, we used to go out at night and shoot any Iraqis we saw, women or children, it didn't matter.

"We went hunting for them; just like people here hunt deer during deer season, and it was fun. We killed and sometimes we did more than that. Gerry likes to pretend none of that ever happened, but trust me, it did.

"You think he was better than me, but he was the same, just dumber and less honest about it. We're all killers, Kane, in one degree or another. Everything else in life is just a matter of taste and appetite."

"I don't believe you."

"You'll see. Have you ever smelled flesh as it burns?"

"What?"

"I first smelled flesh burning in Iraq, during the war. When flesh burns, it smells sweet. Flesh burns sweet and it tastes even sweeter. You'll soon see."

"No! Listen to me, Jeff, don't do this!"

Gilday picked up a sharp knife and stood behind Darcy. He put a bowl down in front of her and held the knife close to her throat with his right hand. He took the young girl by the hair with his left hand and forced her to lean forward over the bowl. Darcy's eyes went wide.

"Let's start the soup."

219

"No!" Kane screamed.

Gilday touched the edge of the blade to Darcy's throat.

Glass broke somewhere in another part of the school.

Gilday put the knife down and listened closely. He stood up.

"Company. Thorne must have gotten my fax. This could make things interesting."

"We're in the kitchen, help!" Kane yelled.

Gilday put the duct tape back on Kane's mouth. Gilday took his pistol out of the holster on his hip and checked it. Reaching behind Kane, he pressed play on a portable CD player on the counter. The Bon Jovi song, "Living On A Prayer," began to play.

"Don't go anywhere. I'll be right back."

Gilday turned off the lights in the kitchen and disappeared.

CHAPTER 50

Thorne and Johnson climbed through a broken classroom window on the first floor. The front end of the snowmobile jutted halfway through the window. At a loss for a way in, Thorne simply aimed the vehicle at the nearest, largest window.

The snow had drifted up high enough against the building that they even had to step down in order to get in. The wind blew snow into the room and blew colored cardboard paper everywhere.

"Are we going to get in trouble for this?" Johnson asked, eyeing the mess.

"Shhh."

Thorne drew his weapon and walked carefully to the classroom door. Johnson followed him awkwardly, bumping into one the lockers lining the wall of the classroom. Thorne glared at him and Johnson mouthed an apology.

Thorne very carefully opened the classroom door and looked both ways down the dark hallway of the school. Thorne took a few steps into the hall and stopped suddenly.

Johnson ran into him. Thorne swiveled and pointed a warning finger at him.

"Johnson!"

"I'm sorry, I didn't …"

"Shut up," Thorne cut him off with a whisper. Music played from somewhere in the school. He looked around and then pointed at Johnson again.

"Stay here."

"Okay."

Thorne started to go, then stopped.

"Johnson."

"What?"

"Draw your weapon."

Johnson clumsily pulled his pistol out from under the snow-clothes he wore.

"Stay here, don't make any noise and don't wander around. You see anybody that isn't me or Kane, don't talk, just shoot them, got it?"

"Yeah, okay, you got it."

Thorne looked at him hard for a moment and then carefully stalked down the darkened hallway, his weapon out in front of him. Hunting.

CHAPTER 51

Darcy Mullens stared at Kane, eyes filled with tears and pleading. Bon Jovi wailed on the stereo. Kane strained her arms against the handcuffs behind her, testing them. Kane knew what she had to do and she wasn't looking forward to it.

Kane took several deep breaths through her nose, positioned her right hand and made her fist as small as possible. Focusing her concentration, Kane wrenched her right hand right through the handcuff, which left skin and blood and dislocated her thumb with an audible pop. Kane screamed in pain through the tape covering her mouth.

Bringing her hands out in front her, the handcuffs still hanging from her left, Kane examined her swollen, damaged right hand and thumb.

Glancing at Darcy, Kane took a couple more deep breaths, preparing herself for what must come next, and then quickly jammed her right thumb back into its socket with another pop. Kane let loose with another muffled scream.

She took the tape off of her mouth, her breath heavy, cold sweat running down her forehead and over her entire body.

Kane untied Darcy and thought hard on how to get her out of this alive.

CHAPTER 52

J ohnson inched out of the classroom and looked
down the hallway. It was long, dark and spooky. It
made Johnson nervous, being in a school at night,
like he was doing something very forbidden. Thorne
seemed to have disappeared; one minute he was there, the
next he was gone. Just like that.

Johnson tiptoed down the hallway trying to see if he
could see where Thorne went. Johnson stopped to admire
the holiday murals on the wall created by the school kids.
The entire wall was covered with artwork.

Johnson followed the murals down the hall. It's good
stuff, Johnson thought. He didn't remember getting to do
this kind of thing when he was in elementary school. Totally
engrossed in the artwork, Johnson came to a turn in the
hallway and almost ran right into Gilday, coming from the
other direction. Both men jumped, startled. They stared at
each other for a moment, and then both laughed,
embarrassed.

"Jesus, Bill," Gilday said. "You about gave me a goddamn
heart attack."

Gilday lowered his weapon and returned it to the holster on his hip. He shook his head good-humoredly.

"You? I think I just lost ten years of my life," Johnson lowered his gun and held his other hand over his heart. "Shit."

"This is the kind of scare that can make a guy's hair fall out prematurely," Gilday said and casually walked to the small "In Case Of Fire" glass case on the wall of the hallway. He opened the door of the case.

"Yeah, tell me about it. What are, uh … what are you doing here anyway, Jeff?"

"That's funny, Bill, 'cause …"

Gilday took the fire ax out of its glass case, turned, swung and smoothly buried it right into Johnson's left side. Blood spattered against the hallway wall.

Johnson was too surprised to even move or cry out, he simply stood there with an ax in his side, blood flecked on his lips, and looked at Gilday in shock. Johnson dropped his weapon to the floor.

"I was about to ask you the same exact thing."

Johnson tried to speak but was unable.

"Shh," Gilday put a finger to his lips. He pulled his weapon back out of his holster and glanced both ways down the hall. "I want to surprise him."

Johnson toppled to the floor, landing on his right side on top of his gun. Blood poured out of his side, as Johnson lay gasping for breath. Gilday left him lying there, ax lodged in his body.

CHAPTER 53

Kane, Darcy in her arms, made her way out of the kitchen quietly as possible and looked for a way out of the school. Darcy sobbed, her face buried into Kane's neck.

"Shhh, I know, honey, we have to be quiet now, shh," Kane whispered to Darcy as she felt her way along in the dark hallway, every closed classroom door hiding a potential threat.

We need to get out and get out quick, Kane thought. Problem one, I'm not sure which way is out. Problem two, we are also both barefoot. No shoes, no parkas, we won't last very long once we do get outside, she thought to herself grimly.

Problem three, I'm not armed. Problem four, we keep running around here we're bound to bump back into Gilday. The school was only one story high but spread out over a large area, like a lot of schools in the Midwest where there was more land than money, with hallways that seem to circle around on each other.

Other than getting out, the only other option was finding

whoever it was that had spooked Gilday. She hoped it was Thorne.

Kane spotted an exit door and ran to it as quietly as she could. The door was chained and locked. Kane pushed and pulled on it as hard as she could to no avail. She forgot about her injured hand and banged on the door with her swollen fist, sending jolts of pain up to her shoulder. Goddamn it, Kane thought, the doors should open from this side as per fire codes.

Gritting her teeth, Kane shifted Darcy to the floor and, holding each other's hands, they quietly returned to the hallway and crept along, looking for another way out.

CHAPTER 54

T horne came to the kitchen and surveyed the setup before him. The grill, left on and still hot, the food preparations and the duct tape. Thorne noted the blood on the floor under Kane's chair.

"Fucker," he whispered to himself. Where the fuck was Kane? Thorne thought.

Thorne unzipped his winter parka to free his movements. Thorne turned off the CD player and the Bon Jovi song ceased.

"I'll show him music," he muttered. This was going to be a hunt, no doubt. The Iceman held the advantage, knew the environment and knew he was being pursued.

Thorne saw something standing in a corner and it gave him an idea.

CHAPTER 55

Kane heard something and hoped it was something good. The wind howled louder down along this part of the hallway, like a door was left open. This could be their out. Kane and Darcy made their way slowly along the hall until they came to a classroom door left open. Peeking in, Kane saw the large hole in the window with a snowmobile teetering in the center. Hope jumped in her heart, hope that she just might get the girl out of this alive.

Before Kane and Darcy could enter, another classroom door two rooms down the hall opened slowly with a creak. Kane and Darcy froze, too afraid to move. The shadow of a man's profile in a snow parka appeared in the window of the classroom door. Parka? He's wearing a parka! Kane thought.

"Thorne?" Kane whispered.

"Kane?" Thorne answered.

Sudden gunfire erupted from behind Kane and shattered the window of the classroom door where Thorne had been standing, the shots hitting him right in the head. Thorne went down.

Kane turned. Gilday stood down at the far end of the hall,

gun at his side. He stood stark still for a moment and then ran toward them. Gilday fired and the bullet bounced off of the wall. Darcy screamed. They ducked into the classroom and Kane slammed the door shut behind them.

Gilday ran to the classroom and threw open the door. Panned his weapon back and forth. He moved swiftly toward the broken window with the snowmobile lodged in the center. Peering out into the storm, he saw no one.

Gilday put his hands on the window and pulled himself up, balancing carefully on the heavy snowmobile. Gilday started to climb out of the window but stopped himself. He stepped back down quietly and slowly backed away, looking at the row of desks to his right, listening.

He stopped beside the third desk down. Gilday tipped the desk over with a quick sudden motion. Darcy, hiding underneath the desk, screamed in terror as Gilday grabbed her by the hair.

Kane exploded from her hiding spot in an opposite locker. Gilday got a shot off, nicking her shoulder. Kane hit him full on with her body before he could fire again. Gilday stumbled backward. He didn't let go of Darcy or his weapon.

Kane grabbed his weapon hand and they wrestled for it, falling through the doorway of the classroom and out into the hallway. With a scream, Kane drove Gilday into the opposite wall. She elbowed him in the face twice and he released Darcy.

"RUN!" Kane screamed.

Darcy fell to the floor, only able to crab away backwards. Kane grabbed Gilday by the hair and brought his head down right into her knee. Gilday's nose broke wetly and his weapon flew from his hand, landing a few feet away.

He punched Kane in the gut, grabbed her damaged hand and squeezed. She screamed. Gilday threw her into the wall and backhanded her across the face. Weak and dazed, she fell to the ground.

"You know what I'm gonna do to you? I'm gonna cut off parts of your own body and make you EAT THEM!" Gilday screamed. He kicked her. Kane lay there, bleeding and beaten.

"Stick a fork in her, Jeff. She's done."

Gilday spun around.

Thorne stood in the hall, not even fifteen feet away, pistol pointed at Gilday. Thorne's snow parka, wrapped about a coatrack, lay on the floor in front of the classroom door with the shot-out window. Thorne had used it as a decoy.

"Very clever," Gilday said. "I should have known better."

"You got that right, sport."

Gilday eyed his own weapon just a foot away on the floor.

"How'd you find me?"

Kane crabbed away from Gilday in the opposite direction until she came to the turn in the hallway. Thorne's pistol didn't waver from Gilday.

"Where else does one go to be taught?"

"Caught that, did ya?"

"Pathetically easy."

"Are gonna take me in, cowboy?"

"Nope."

Kane almost ran into Johnson, still alive and crawling toward her at the hall intersection, a trail of blood behind him, ax still stuck in his side. He looked at Kane, his face white and drawn, and tried to speak.

"So all that you said about how taking the guy in as the only way to let him know that you won, that was all bullshit?"

"You already know that I've won."

"Don't you want to know why I did it?" Gilday was careful not to move an inch.

"I already know why."

Thorne pulled the trigger on his pistol, but it wouldn't fire. He tried again.

"You're not used to cold weather, are you?" Gilday chuckled. "Subzero temperatures can cause the slide on a Glock to stick, it's a real bitch," Gilday suddenly made a move for his weapon.

Thorne lowered his pistol and frantically worked the slide with his left hand. Gilday reached his weapon on the floor and knelt down to pick it up.

Thorne finally got the slide to move and chambered a bullet. Gilday got his hand on his weapon.

He looked at Gilday and Gilday looked at him.

They both brought their weapons up, drawing like the westerns of old, and fired. Gilday, kneeling on the floor, was just a little faster. Gilday shot Thorne in the upper left part of his chest. Thorne's bullet whizzed by Gilday's head an inch too far to the right.

Thorne dropped his weapon as he hit the ground, bleeding. Gilday sauntered over to where Thorne lay on the floor, his back against the wall. Thorne struggled to reach his weapon. Gilday kicked it away and pointed his gun right at Thorne's face.

"You're no Shane," he said to Thorne.

Gilday chambered a round.

"Hey, Jeff."

Gilday turned. Kane buried the fire ax right into his chest.

Gilday stumbled back into the wall opposite Thorne, blood spraying everywhere, and slid slowly down the wall. Kane kicked his weapon away.

She knelt down in front of Thorne, who struggled to sit up.

"I can't believe this, I'm losing it, I must be really losing it," Thorne mumbled.

"Hold still, be quiet," Kane said to him.

"I must be getting fucking old."

"It's better than the alternative. Hold this here."

Kane took the stocking cap off of Thorne's head and put it on the wound to his chest. She took Thorne's hand and put it over the cap. They looked at each other for a moment. Thorne winked.

Gilday gurgled. Kane turned and stood before him. He tried to speak but couldn't, blood bubbling out of his mouth. Kane leaned in close.

"I already knew blood came out hot," she whispered quietly to him.

Darcy suddenly appeared right beside Kane, startling her. Darcy took Kane's hand into hers.

"Was he a bad man?" Darcy asked.

"Yes, honey. He was a real bad man."

Just to make sure it was over for good, Darcy and Kane both watched as Gilday slowly and painfully died.

CHAPTER 56

Kane sat on a couch in the den of Thorne's cozy and very secure house up in the woods of Virginia a few weeks later. It was a very nice den, wood panels and comfortable couch, bar in one corner. A lot more style to his place than she would have originally guessed, Kane thought, at least judging by the way he dressed.

Old school rat pack type of vibe, that's what it was, she decided. If he ever decided to stop dressing like a caustic English Lit professor, he might be worth considering.

Thorne, his shoulder bandaged and his arm in a sling, set a chessboard down on the coffee table in front of her and a box of carved chess pieces. Thorne had slowly regained the use of his arm and didn't really need the sling, but was under doctor's orders to take it easy and not to overtax the arm.

Kane had gotten out of the hospital with a cast on her right wrist and hand, various bruises on her body and a complete sense of satisfaction.

Kane dug the pieces out of the box and started to set the board up. Thorne moved to his vast and expensive stereo system. He'd decided that the best song to start this evening off with would be Sarah Vaughan's "No 'Count Blues."

"Pete was telling me how fortunate I am to get invited to the great Jacob Thorne's house, he said you never let anyone come up here," Kane said.

"Nobody he knows, anyway."

"By the way, Johnson's gonna make it; he won't able to walk but he's gonna pull through."

"Who?"

"Johnson. Bill Johnson. The cop on the snowmobile with you. Jesus Christ."

"Oh yeah, him. Hey! Be careful! Those pieces are valuable antiques, you can't just bounce them around like it's your diaphragm on a Saturday night."

"So listen, Jake …"

"Jake?"

"After all we've been through, I can't call you Jake?"

"No," Thorne sat down comfortably opposite Kane.

"I saved your life."

"And I can't tell you how disappointed I am with myself in that regard."

Thorne grabbed the queens off of the board and turned away from Kane in order to hide them. He presented both closed fists to Kane. She picked his right hand. It held the white queen. Kane took the queens and put them in their places.

"So listen, Jake," Kane continued after a moment, "is Pete going give you another crack at Kevorkian and the Mercy Killings?"

"Eventually."

"You going to catch him?"

"Eventually."

"Can I work the Mercy Killings with you?"

"Nope."

"Why not?

"You got the shakes."

"Not anymore. And not when I'm holding an ax," Kane raised her eyebrow at him and smiled. "You know what happened?"

"Let me guess. No shakes."

"Not a one. They're gone."

"How nice for you."

"So can I work Kevorkian with you?"

Thorne studied her a moment. He leaned forward.

"Answer this question."

"What?"

"How did it feel, the day you shot and killed those piece of shit rapists in the van?"

"The same as it felt when I killed the Iceman."

"Describe this feeling."

"You want to know what it felt like?"

"I want to know what it felt like for you."

"Good," Kane said after a moment. "It felt good."

"It felt good."

"It felt REAL good," Kane leaned back, remembering. "Too good, even."

"And that's what scared you, how good it felt?"

"It was scary. I liked how good it felt. I liked it so much that it scared me."

Thorne looked at her for a moment and then broke into a large smile.

"What?" Kane asked.

Thorne stood, went behind his bar and grabbed a couple of glasses. He brought them back to the table and returned to the bar.

"What? Why are you looking at me with that big shit-eating grin on your face?" Kane asked.

"I got a bottle of twenty-five-year-old scotch back here. I

am going to pour the two of us a big stiff drink of world-class hooch."

Thorne took a key from his pocket and unlocked a cabinet. He took a bottle of scotch out of the cabinet and set it on top of the bar. He stared at Kane for another moment, still grinning.

"Does this mean I'm working Kevorkian with you?"

"I think I'm starting to like you, Kane," Thorne knelt back down behind the bar and unlocked another, much larger cabinet located underneath.

"You are? You're starting to like me?"

"Yep," Thorne replied, his head buried deep inside the lower cabinet.

"And is that a good thing?"

Inside the large cabinet were rows and rows of small jars, each one labeled and filled with medical alcohol. There were over two hundred of the tiny jars labeled with names and dates lined up in the cabinet.

Human tongues floated inside of them.

On the end of one of the top rows there were empty jars. One of the empty jars was labeled FORSYTHE. Another empty was labeled PETE.

Thorne grabbed an empty jar labeled KANE, took it out, locked the cabinet and stood back up.

"What's that you said?" Thorne asked.

"I said, is that a good thing, you liking me?"

"It's a good thing."

Thorne tore the "KANE" label off the jar and tossed it into a waste can. He set the jar aside, picked up the bottle of scotch and brought it back to the table.

"An extremely good thing. I don't like most people," Thorne poured both of them a drink.

"Yeah, I've noticed that about you."

They tapped each other's glass in a silent toast and sipped their scotch.

"This is good hooch," Kane said, savoring the scotch. "I'm beginning to think that you might actually have some taste, Thorne."

Thorne smiled gently at Kane.

"White moves first, Emma."

Kane made her opening move with a pawn. Thorne countered her immediately. Kane made another quick move and Thorne again countered quickly. Emma Kane smiled at Jacob Thorne.

"I can see that this is going to be really interesting," Kane said.

"You have no idea."

EPILOGUE

T HE END.

BUT WAIT... check the next page... heh-heh-heh...

Todd Travis is an independently published author. He created Emma Kane / Jacob Thorne because he has always been a serious fan of psychological thrillers and serial killer fiction and wanted more books in the genre to exist. He wrote Creatures of Appetite in his spare time on a dare from a friend, as a result the worm escaped the Tequila bottle and his life has been forever changed. There are currently three books in this series... the next two are:

TROPHIES - Emma Kane / Jacob Thorne Book 2
TALENTS - Emma Kane / Jacob Thorne Book 3

More of their adventures are on the way. If you enjoy Emma and Jacob's adventures, you can pitch in and support his work. Todd accepts donations, just go to:

Chip in HERE to Keep Todd Writing

Donate whatever you can spare. One dollar, two or three. Todd puts whatever he makes from sales and donations right back into the books, this is a labor of love for him. Toss him a couple-three bucks to keep him in coffee and anger management classes.

Please leave reviews whenever you can. And thank you for your kind support of an indie author.

A special shout-out of thanks to Team Travis, the secret runners who help get this work into shape of public eyes. They're all important, but on this particular update, Kristy E and Dan H went above and beyond.

EMMA KANE & JACOB THORNE
RETURN IN...

TROPHIES...

Young beautiful women are disappearing. Different types, with
different backgrounds, most with a lot of debt, few friends and no
close family to speak of. Gone.

Someone is collecting trophies. Only one person can see it. Special
Agent Emma Kane.

Kane knows she'll need help on this ordeal. But the only man who
can help her, famed profiler Jacob Thorne, is no longer speaking to
her. The clock is ticking and Kane is now a target of whomever is
doing this.

As Kane gets closer to unlocking true cruel purpose the abducted
women serve, the real question is not only will she survive what she
finds, but can she handle what she discovers about Thorne and
herself?

Emma Kane and Jacob Thorne are back in this thrilling sequel to
Todd Travis' pulse-pounding debut novel **CREATURES OF
APPETITE**.

TROPHIES - Emma Kane / Jacob Thorne Book 2
a novel by Todd Travis.

TALENTS

In 1989, a school bus filled with young children disappears. It drove into a tunnel, a tunnel with no exits, and did not drive out. Witnesses saw the bus go in. No one saw it come out. It vanished into thin air as a community panics. Everyone panics.

Everyone except for a twenty-four year old college dropout named Jacob Thorne.

In 2004, three people are brutally murdered, two of them in a sealed panic room, a room locked from the inside.

The only trace evidence is a single hair from the suspect. A suspect that has been dead for three months, killed by the same people who were just murdered in the panic room.

Everyone is convinced a ghost has come back from the grave to avenge a murder.

Everyone except for a young PTSD-suffering homicide detective named Emma Kane.

To be a profiler, it takes more than just research and hard work. It takes more than simply brains.

It takes... TALENT.

And you need to have it from the very beginning.

TALENTS - Emma Kane / Jacob Thorne Book 3.

An origin story of two very unique people.

ALSO BY TODD TRAVIS:

A geek. A fat chick. A slow learner. A psycho suicide girl. A wannabe criminal. Five outcast high school kids with nothing in common except that nobody liked them. Five losers with nothing to look forward to but torment and harassment every day; nothing, that is, until they were introduced to the game.

SEX, MARRY, KILL.

An online game that would change their lives and give them power over others. They could do anything they wanted, sleep with anyone they wanted to, kill anyone who got in their way. Their every fantasy fulfilled. But at a mortal price. They soon discover that game will consume and destroy them unless they find some way to stop it before it's too late.

For fans of Stephen King and Joe Hill, a dark tale of horror, revenge and gaming gone lethally wrong. **SEX, MARRY, KILL.**

ALSO BY TODD TRAVIS

For fans of STEPHEN KING and DEAN KOONTZ ... author
TODD TRAVIS (Creatures of Appetite) has gathered a haunting
collection of suspense stories exploring the monsters, both living
and dead, which surround us all.

- A brilliant biophysicist on the verge of proving there is no life after
death discovers, to his horror, that the dead are determined to
stop him ...

- An abused small town boy finds a special friend in the woods next
to his trailer, but his friend isn't like other children and cannot leave
the woods, not ever ...

- A group of determined graduate students seek Bigfoot on a remote
Alaskan range seek but discover a monster far more deadly than
they ever imagined ...

- An elderly store manager, disturbed by a stranger eyeing the
armored truck deliveries to his store, decides to take matters into
his own hands ...

- A beautiful young woman walks the streets of Manhattan at night
seeking men, but for her own dark purposes, because for her, night
is for hunting ...

- A mysterious little girl somehow "invites" herself along on an
abduction, leading her captors to wonder who really is in charge ...

Five stories of suspense and terror and a short novel exploring the
darkness everyone eventually faces when it's their time to die, THE
LIVING AND THE DEAD is a collection one may want to read
with all the lights in the house on ...

THE LIVING AND THE DEAD

<u>DERELICT</u>

All Kathleen Castle cares about is making the latest payment on her beloved boat, a salvager named DADDY'S GIRL, and not falling back into a bottle of vodka.

But when she and her all-female crew answer a mysterious distress call during a tropical storm, they stumble across an abandoned yacht worth millions.

It seems like a dream come true, the Lotto, the Big Ticket to all their dreams...

Until they discover what's waiting for them inside the ship...

<u>DERELICT</u>

A horror novella

by

Todd Travis

ABOUT THE AUTHOR

Todd Travis' interests include conspiracy theories, the poetry of Michael O'Donoghue and pop music and movies of the 80s. He is single and moves around a lot. His current whereabouts are at this time unknown. He dislikes cable news, views cell phones with suspicion and don't even get him started on email. He also believes poker is not a sport and therefore should never be allowed on ESPN.

CREATURES OF APPETITE is his first novel. The sequel, **TROPHIES**, launched in 2016, and another Kane / Thorne novel **TALENTS** arrived in 2017.

More are on the way. There is a Facebook fan page started by one of his very few friends. Check there for updates or messages. **Novelist Todd Travis**.

He is an independently published novelist. You can support his work by donating a dollar or three at this link:

Chip in HERE to Keep Todd Writing

Note to readers: Thank you for your support, and if you have the time, please share that support by leaving reviews for the books wherever they can be found, Amazon, Goodreads, etc. Every review matters, every reviewer counts. Thanks.